Mr. Spangler,

I do not know if you are going to understand what I am about to do. I do not know if I understand it myself, but I am leaving Juneau City at the end of the week and will be heading to Colorado. It makes no sense, but lately I have been homesick for a place I have never been and I have been missing a boy I have never seen. The yearning I read in John James's letters is the yearning I have felt my whole life. It is a need to be important to someone. And I aim to be that to the boy if I am able.

I want to make a difference in your great-grandson's life. By the time you get this, you will not be able to reach me, and you could not have said anything that would have changed my mind anyhow. I am on my way to meet John James. This is something I need to do. I want your great-grandson to have what every boy deserves—a father who cares about him.

Sincerely,

Wesley M. Burrows

* * *

### *Her Colorado Man*
**Harlequin® Historical #971—December 2009**

M

# CHERYL St. John

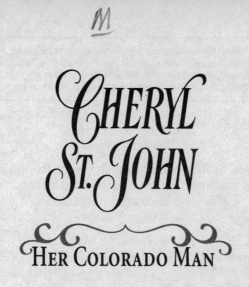

## HER COLORADO MAN

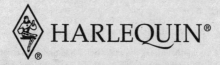

# HARLEQUIN®

TORONTO • NEW YORK • LONDON
AMSTERDAM • PARIS • SYDNEY • HAMBURG
STOCKHOLM • ATHENS • TOKYO • MILAN • MADRID
PRAGUE • WARSAW • BUDAPEST • AUCKLAND

Recycling programs
for this product may
not exist in your area.

ISBN-13: 978-0-373-29571-5

HER COLORADO MAN

Copyright © 2009 by Cheryl Ludwigs.

**Printed in U.S.A.**

As most writers can attest, this rewarding job often takes a toll on hands, wrists, elbows, necks, shoulders and backs. I am deeply appreciative of Dr. Steven Shockley, who has adjusted my spine more times than I could say, and who instructs me in methods of exercise to attain optimal wellness. I'm not the only one who has a better quality of life because this dedicated chiropractor is concerned with helping patients achieve natural drug-free healing. Thank you, Dr. Steve, for your genuine compassion and for sharing your gifts and abilities.

# Chapter One

Ruby Creek, Colorado
May, 1882

"Watch out!"

Mariah Burrows ducked and ran a good six feet before turning back to look up at the crate teetering atop a stack of similar ones in the cavernous warehouse. Three agile young men scrambled from their positions on ladders and beside wagons to prevent it from falling. Two of them were her nephews, the other a distant cousin.

"Don't stack these crates over twelve high," she called. "Better that we take up warehouse space than lose eighty-five dollars or someone's head. We built this whole building just for storing the lager for the Exposition, so let's use it."

Her nephew Roth gave her a mock salute and jumped

down from the pile of wooden crates. "Grandpa would've had our hides if we'd let that one slip."

"I'd have told your mother not to serve that *apfel-strudel* you're so fond of tonight."

He laughed and took his cap from his rear pocket to settle it on his head. "You're a tyrannical boss, Aunt Mariah."

"Mariah!" A familiar male voice echoed through the high-ceilinged building. "Mariah Burrows!"

"Over here, Wilhelm," she called. At twenty-two, he was her younger brother by two years. He used her full name at every opportunity. Among the hundred plus employees at the Spangler Brewery, hers was one of the few non-Bavarian or German names, and he lived to tease her about it. "What has you out of the office this morning?" she asked.

"Grandfather wants to see you right away."

She fished for her pencil in the front pocket of the men's trousers she wore that were her everyday garb. "I'll be there as soon as I go over the inventory of last night's bottling."

"No, right now. He says it's urgent."

She tucked her ledger under her arm and rushed to join him. "Is John James all right?"

"Your son is fine."

"Grandfather?"

"He's just anxious to have you in the office for whatever reason."

Relieved, she turned to wave at Roth. "I'll be back.

Go ahead and start stamping those crates near the conveyor. Seven weeks until opening day in Denver."

Spangler Brewery spread over an acre located roughly two miles from Ruby Creek. The warehouses were situated with platforms a few scant feet from the railroad tracks, and the production buildings sat close to the cold-water streams that poured from the mountains into the wide creek for which the town was named. Three smoke stacks puffed billowy gray clouds into the bright Colorado sky. The mountains to the northeast were still capped with snow, but fireweed and forget-me-nots bloomed on the hillsides nearer. Mariah breathed in the pungent smell of fermented hops.

"I overheard Mama talking in the kitchen this morning." Wilhelm's tone was uncharacteristically solemn.

She glanced up at him as they passed the corner of the four-sided brick clock tower that stood in the center of the open yard.

"She said that sometimes Grandpa forgets what day it is for a moment."

Mariah had noticed the same thing a time or two. Once he'd said something about an occurrence twenty years ago as if it had just happened. But the next moment he carried on with their business. "He seems perfectly healthy," she said. "It's almost like he takes a little trip into the past."

"No harm there, I guess," her brother said with a shrug.

Near the front entrance, they entered the four-story brick building that housed accounting offices as well as comfortable quarters for her grandfather. Their work shoes padded on the carpet runner that ran the length of the hall.

Mariah smiled a goodbye to Wilhelm and opened one of the carved walnut doors to enter Louis Spangler's domain. She'd loved these rooms from the time she'd been a child, when he'd indulgently welcomed her to sit in one of the soft leather chairs that sat before a stone fireplace. She'd listened with rapt attention as he spoke of the old days back in Bavaria and his early days in this country, when he and his father and his uncles had built the brewery from the ground up.

He was the only one left from the old country. He and Grandma used to speak to each other in Old High German, a dialect of which their children and grandchildren could only understand bits and phrases. Mariah hadn't heard it spoken for many years now.

"You must need something important," she said. "You've spent the last three months cautioning me not to waste a minute until everything is ready for the Exposition."

Louis moved from where he'd been standing at the wide window that looked out over foothills decorated in a dozen shades of verdant green to his desk. He cast her a tentative glance. "We have something important to discuss."

"About the Exposition?"

"No. Nothing like that." He waved her to a chair.

Mariah knew better than to rush him. He would come

around to the point in his own good time. She made herself comfortable on a wing chair and waited. The concern in his vivid blue gaze unsettled her.

"I have some news. Something that's going to affect you and John James."

She sat a little straighter. Four years ago he'd given her a seat on the governing board, and for the first time in its nearly forty-year history, the brewery had a woman in a principal position. He'd always held Mariah in a place of favor. When her son had come along, Grandfather had given him his favor, as well. She anticipated that one day she would inherit her own share of their family holdings. "What is it?" she asked.

"Wes Burrows is coming here. In just a few weeks' time."

Mariah heard his spoken words immediately, but their meaning took longer to penetrate her haze of disbelief. They never spoke of the person he'd just mentioned because that person didn't exist. Hearing it from him now was like hearing that foreign language her grandparents used to use. "Wha-what do you mean?"

"John James's father is coming to see him."

A buzz rang in her ears. "But that—that's impossible."

"I'm afraid it's not. I've had communication with him, and he's already left Juneau City. He should arrive early next month."

Mariah's first reaction was to stand. Bolt perhaps. But the room tilted at an odd angle, and she collapsed back onto the leather cushion before she fell. "Could you explain, please? How does a man you invented suddenly write and say he's coming?"

"I didn't invent Wes Burrows. The man exists."

She overcame her light-headedness to stand and release the tension ratcheting her nerves by pacing a few feet away and back again. "I thought your old friend from Forchheim was writing those letters."

"Otto died. I told you that."

"No. No, you didn't." Just the other day she'd read a few of the letters her son had received recently, and there had been subtle differences in the penmanship and the sentence structures, but she hadn't suspected a different writer.

Mariah placed a hand on either side of her head as though to keep it from flying off. Was her grandfather confused or was she hearing wrong? "If Otto is dead, who has been writing to—and who is traveling to—see John James?"

"I didn't expect this," he said apologetically. "Not in a hundred years. Sit back down and let me explain."

He wouldn't continue until she complied, so Mariah sat once again and gripped the arms of the chair. "I'm listening."

"Otto Weiss had been living in Alaska for quite some time when I asked him to help us with the name of someone who rarely checked his postal box, someone whose name we could use and who would never find out."

"I know that part." Seven years ago, when she'd told him she was going to have a baby and had no plans for a husband, he'd sent her to Chicago for a year. She'd been surprised when she'd returned home with her baby and learned that her grandfather had invented a husband for her while she'd been away. The story had already been told throughout the family and in the nearby town of Ruby Creek. Supposedly she'd married in Chicago.

The tale continued that her new husband had gone off to the gold fields of the north, leaving her to wait for him, and because of that she'd chosen to move home to her family until his return.

Living with the stigma of a husband with gold fever had been better than her son or anyone else learning the truth. Louis had found a solution. A no-muss, no-fuss absent husband suited Mariah just fine actually. The ruse had kept away potential suitors and given her the freedom to live her life exactly the way she pleased. A pretend husband had been an easy solution.

"Alaska is at the edge of nowhere," he said. "I never dreamed anyone in Colorado would hear Burrows's name."

When he'd shown her the first letter from this make-believe father, he had suggested that his friend would write and send a few letters so John James could believe his father loved him. "A boy needs to believe his father cares for him," he'd told Mariah. She hadn't been able to disagree with that. And the truth would never pass her lips. "All along I thought Otto made up a name to use," she said.

"We should have simply rented a box in a fictitious name," her grandfather said. "Or we should have said your husband died like we talked about, but John James loved getting those letters. Telling him that would have been like actually killing his father. He believed the man was real. At the time there was no harm in allowing the ruse to continue."

"I'm as responsible as you are for that," she said. "But what about the name that I've been using—the name I gave my son? This *Burrows* is a real person?"

"He is."

The information was too much to absorb. Thinking back, she had noticed a difference in the letters. She hadn't read all of them, but she read a few here and there for John James's safety. She'd read more than usual lately because she'd been intrigued by the writer's stories. "Who are the letters really from?"

"The real Mr. Burrows. Initially he wrote to me because I always help John James with his letters. He asked me to explain why his post box was filled with mail from a child he didn't know. I made it clear how much the dear boy longed for a father." He gave her a sidelong glance. "I may have suggested that no harm would come if the charade continued a while longer. And soon this Burrows fellow was writing letters to John James."

Mariah wiped a hand over her eyes as if that might clear the confusion and concern. "Why didn't you tell me?"

"I did." He frowned and his gaze fell to the desktop. "Or at least I thought I did."

Her heart beat hard and fast at the thought of this stranger coming to expose their lie to her son. John

James's heart would be broken. He would despise her for the lies she'd strung out for so long. A tight knot formed in her stomach at the thought, and suspicion straightened her eyebrows in a skeptical frown. "Why does this man want to come here? What does he expect?"

Louis unlocked his top desk drawer and took out an envelope. He tapped it against his other palm thoughtfully before placing it on top of his desk and pushing it toward her. "It's all here."

With trembling fingers, Mariah reached for the envelope. Her grandfather's name had been written in sprawling black script. She slid out the stationery and unfolded the paper.

Mr. Spangler,

I do not know if you are going to understand what I am about to do. I do not know if I understand it myself, but I am leaving Juneau City at the end of the week and will be heading to Colorado.

For the past six years, I have been traveling between tent camps and post offices. There is money to be made in this land, and I have spent my youth acquiring it. I have witnessed plenty of men getting mail from home, and I have often wondered what it would be like to have family waiting for me, wishing I was with them.

Before I was a mail carrier, I worked aboard a whaling ship. I once tried my luck at gold mining, and I have traveled half the world. In all that time I never felt attached to a place. I never had a yearning to settle until I read the lad's words about the Spangler family. He writes about his mother and you. I feel as though I have been to Ruby Creek.

It makes no sense, but lately I have been homesick for a place I have never been and I have been missing a boy I have never seen. The yearning I read in John James's letters is the yearning I have felt my whole life. It is a need to be important to someone. And I aim to be that to him if I am able.

I have had some time to reflect on my life these past weeks, and what I now see is that above all I want to make a difference in this world. I want to make a difference in your great-grandson's life. By the time you get this, you will not be able to reach me, and you could not have said anything that would have changed my mind anyhow. I am on my way to meet John James.

You have my word that I shall not embarrass or hurt the boy. Neither do I intend to disrupt your life or your granddaughter's. This is something I need to do. I want your great-grandson to have what every boy deserves—a father who cares about him.

Sincerely, Wesley T. Burrows

Hot tears stung at the backs of Mariah's eyes. Fear and resentment welled up strong and fierce. The words written in black ink blurred in her vision. Blinking, she folded the letter and slid it back into the envelope. "This is absurd. We don't know this man. What right does he have to come galloping in here like a savior on a white horse and weasel his way into our lives?"

Standing, she tossed the envelope back on his desk and walked behind her chair. She grasped the leather in both hands in an attempt to stop her violent trembling. "What are we going to do?"

Her grandfather stood and made his way around the corner of the enormous walnut desk. "There's nothing we can do. We used his postal box for several years without his permission. He's caught us in a lie."

"Which gives him the power to come in here and *ruin our lives?*" she exclaimed. "What if he's coming to blackmail us? What better reason could he have to travel across a continent to intrude on our family?"

"Blackmail? That's a pretty big leap. I've read his other letters to John James, and I don't believe he means us any harm. We'll deal with anything that comes up when the time arrives, Mariah. There's no call to jump to conclusions."

"No." Panic rose in her chest. "You can have someone stop him before he gets here."

"Who would I ask to deter him? Your brothers? Your nephews? Just what would I tell them? And what would we do with Burrows once we'd stopped him? He's not breaking any laws by coming here."

Mariah didn't like feeling trapped, and she didn't like

anyone having the control over her that this Wes Burrows had at the moment. The man was up to no good. "No one has ever seen him," she said. "When he gets here, we'll say he's an imposter."

"Mariah, that would—"

"I know—it would raise too many questions and still create a scene for John James." She paced several feet away and then walked back to face her grandfather.

"I'm going to take his words at face value," Louis said. "He wants John James to know he has a father who cares about him."

"He *doesn't* have a father who cares about him," she said in a tight voice. "I'm not blaming you for anything." She took a step forward and leaned to rest her hand on his shirtsleeve. "When I came back with a baby, I was relieved that you'd already told everyone the story about a husband. It spared me the embarrassment of making explanations. I accepted the lie because it was convenient. And even when Otto sent those first letters, I could have stopped you from giving them to John James, but I didn't." Her throat burned with the truth and the scalding honesty. "I wanted him to believe he had a father."

She swallowed hard and a trembling began in her knees. "This man coming here is taking the lie too far. Even if his intent is harmless, and he pretends to be a father, he'll leave eventually. Desertion will only hurt John James more in the end."

Louis moved his arm to grasp her hand and hold it

between both of his. "Let's say he visits for a few weeks. And then he goes back where he came from. Things will go back like they were and John James will have had a father like all the other children."

"But it's always been a lie." She couldn't push her voice past a whisper because her chest ached too fiercely. Maybe the lie had allowed her to pretend there was someone out there who would be returning one day.

Louis released her and stared out the window. His hair glowed silver in the sunlight. "It's a little late to tell the truth," he said, turning back to level a gaze on her. "Or is there a chance the child's real father will show up one day?"

She looked into his eyes, eyes that had always looked upon her with loving trust and kindness.

The truth would tear her family apart.

With a dull pain in her chest, she shook her head. "No. He'll never show up."

"I've never pressured you, Mariah," he said kindly, and it was true. Nor had he ever condemned her. His love for her had never wavered. "My deepest regret is that you don't trust me with the truth…but I trust you."

"You and my father are the only men on this earth I trust," she said with the acidic taste of guilt on her tongue. But then she repented in her thoughts, because she had four brothers who would die for her at a moment's notice. "Well, there are my brothers, of course…but I don't trust this stranger."

He took several steps to take her in his arms and hold her against his satin vest. He smelled of spice and shaving soap and everything dear and familiar. She had to hold back a sob or drown in a torrent. "Whoever this outsider is, I don't plan to welcome him or treat him kindly," she warned. "Even if he *were* my gadabout husband, no one would expect me to welcome him with open arms after all these years."

"We'll do what we have to," Louis answered. "We'll do what we believe is right for John James."

"Wes Burrows doesn't know what's right for John James. He doesn't even know us." Her voice broke, and she caught herself before she lost her composure. "I'll figure out what he's up to," she said. "And I won't let him hurt my son."

She loved her grandfather with every beat of her heart. He'd meant well. They'd both believed that saving her good name and giving her son an identity was best for him. John James had never suffered the indignity of being born out of wedlock, and she'd been spared shame and embarrassment.

Until now.

# *Chapter Two*

That evening as the sun slid toward the western horizon, Mariah caught a ride home in the back of a company wagon leaving the yard. Her brother Arlen gave her an arm up, and she leaped over the side to take a seat in the bed beside her family members.

Arlen lived in the family home with Grandfather and their parents, as did she and John James, her two younger sisters, a widowed aunt and her cousin Marc's family.

Mariah's family had lived in a separate house once, but when her mother's sight had failed, they'd moved into the big house so Henrietta wasn't alone during the day. Now Wilhelm and his family lived in the house they'd vacated, which was only several hundred feet from this one.

For practicality, all of the Spanglers lived within a half a mile radius of the brewery and each other. Grandfather said it was like having their own Bavarian district.

They shopped, worshipped and visited in Ruby Creek on a regular basis, though, always taking an interest in the community and usually attending church.

The good-natured chatter and teasing between cousins and siblings was lost on her today; her thoughts had been narrowed to one subject—and one person— since that morning.

The wagon slowed and Arlen, along with her cousin Marc, jumped down. Arlen reached back for Mariah's hand and Marc helped his wife to the ground. Faye adjusted her skirts and took his hand as they headed toward the rear entry.

Men and women parted in the yard, the men headed for the washhouse. Mariah followed Faye in through the sun porch to the enormous kitchen filled with mouth-watering aromas. Her aunt Ina turned from one of the steaming cast-iron stoves to welcome them with a smile.

Mariah's mother sat on a wooden stool near a chopping block, peeling potatoes. "Hello, Mama," Mariah greeted her.

"How was your workday?" Henrietta asked and raised her cheek for a kiss.

"It was long." Mariah joined Faye at a deep sink to scrub her hands. "I'll be down to help with supper after I wash up and change."

"There you are!" her cousin Hildy exclaimed when the two of them nearly collided in the doorway. "John James has been waiting for you."

Hildy didn't live with them. She had worked in the brewery for a couple of years, but most recently she'd been a companion to Henrietta. She preferred helping with the household chores and watching over the younger children to a brewery position, and the arrangement suited everyone. Hildy had no children of her own.

"I gave the children toast and eggs after school," Hildy told her. "Though they'd have much preferred your mama's cookies."

"You're a blessing," Mariah told her sweet dark-haired cousin and looked into her hazel eyes. They couldn't have been more different in appearance. Hildy's father had been of Irish decent, while Mariah took after the fair-haired Bavarian Spanglers.

Instead of using the back staircase, she headed for the front of the house and ran up the wide front staircase that opened into a commons room. There, the four youngsters had their own benches, desks, slates and a case of books, as well as an assortment of games and puzzles for evenings and rainy afternoons.

"Mama!" John James leaped up from his position on the rug to hug her. "I added five numbers together in my head without my fingers. Or the slate."

"I do believe you have a calling to work in the accounting office with your uncle Wilhelm." She ruffled his blond hair and knelt to kiss his cheek. He smelled like chalk and soap and little boy, and her heart tripped at the thought of him ever being hurt.

"Oh, no," he said with a shake of his fair head. "I'm going to work on the machines." His blue-eyed expression held all the seriousness a six-year-old could muster. "I like the sounds in the bottling house. And you can see the mountains from the big doorway."

"That you can," she agreed. "You, my bright shining star, can be whatever you want to be when you grow up."

"Even the president?" Marc and Faye's seven-year-old Emma asked, with a grin.

Mariah turned to tweak her pigtail. "Unless you beat him to it!"

"Emma can't be the pwesident!" Emma's five-year-old brother Paul said with a wide-eyed exclamation. "Her's a girl! Pwesident's got to have beards."

Mariah laughed and the boys joined her. Emma only gave them a puzzled look.

"Finish your lessons before supper," she said to John James and hurried along the hallway to her room.

Supper was a noisy affair as always, relaxed and friendly. At home like this she wasn't anyone's boss or coworker. She didn't have a quota or hours and product to tally. She was simply aunt, sister, daughter and mother. Siblings and cousins and aunts and uncles talked over each other while they passed heaping bowls of potatoes and platters of *schweinsbraten,* their traditional oven-roasted pork. Half a dozen foamy pitchers of dark beer stood on the table at intervals.

Mariah set down her empty glass with a satisfied

sigh. Only perfect brews came from the barrels with the Spangler stamp.

Noticing her lack of animation, Mariah's father, Friederick, gave her a long glance. "Are you well, Mariah?"

She assured him she was fine. "It was a long day. I'm just tired."

Much later after the dishes were washed and the various families had retired to their quarters, Mariah tucked John James into his bed in the room he shared with Paul. He closed his eyes and she threaded her fingers through his pale silky hair.

Wesley Burrows's written words came to mind: *I want your great-grandson to have what every boy deserves—a father who cares about him.* No one wished that more than she, but it would never be. Memories of her son as a chubby infant and a toddling two-year-old assailed her. The other children in their household—in all their family—had fathers to swing them in the air and play catch and teach them to fish and hunt.

Her brothers were wonderful, and she loved them for their devotion to her son. Arlen never left with a fishing pole without asking John James if he wanted to accompany him. Mariah often tagged along and watched as her brother taught him how to dig for worms, place one on the hook and cast the line into the stream.

She stretched out on the narrow bed and lay with her face nestled in John James's hair where it met the collar of his nightshirt. He was never lonely. She'd seen to that. Her family had seen to it. She owed them a debt she could never repay for loving her child and giving him a sense of belonging.

He slept soundly, his breath a soft whisper against the cotton sheet.

She was the one who was lonely. She was the one who watched couples with curiosity and awe. She was the one who lay awake at night, knowing she'd never have anything more than what she had at that moment, and vowing that she was going to be satisfied regardless.

She would never marry. She would never have another child. She would never be loved in the way a man loves a woman. It was unlikely she'd ever love a man who wasn't her closest of kin.

Sometimes she thought she could embellish the lie she lived by saying that her husband had been killed. She'd imagined a hundred deaths for him. And if he were dead, she'd be free to be courted. Though she was decidedly unapproachable and rarely met men who weren't her family.

But she couldn't tell that additional lie just for her convenience. The thought of doing that to John James stopped her. As it was he believed he had a father, no matter how distant. If he believed his father was dead, it would hurt him more.

Wouldn't it?

The partially closed door creaked open and Faye

peeked in. Paul had been asleep since before John James came to bed. Mariah couldn't see Faye's gaze, but knew she checked her son before giving Mariah a little wave and backing out.

It didn't matter now. At this point she didn't have any power to alter the husband fable. Wesley Burrows was coming to insinuate himself into their lives. And she was going to have to tell John James.

Mariah got up and went to the bureau that held John James's clothing and opened the bottom drawer. Raising the lid on a hinged wooden cigar box, she lifted out a packet of envelopes tied with a piece of string and left the room, silently closing the door behind her.

Mariah's room was across the hall from where her son slept and beside her brother Arlen's. It was a comfortable space, plenty roomy enough for a big upholstered chair beside the fireplace, a writing desk and the four-poster bed in which she'd slept since childhood. A padded seat had been built before a trio of paned windows that overlooked the vegetable and herb gardens, with forested hills in the background.

Mariah lit another lamp and settled at her desk with the packet of letters. After first identifying the differences between two similar, but individual styles of handwriting, she sorted the envelopes into piles accordingly. These weren't all of the letters, but they were the most recent, dating back nearly a year.

From those with the earliest dates, she scanned a

few, and then set them aside. Starting with the first one after the handwriting changed, she began to read.

Dear John James,

As soon as the weather is warm and the rivers are free of ice so that canoes and steamboats can carry the mail, I will send the book I have been saving for you. It holds many drawings of steam engines, and I believe you will enjoy looking at them. Right now, during the harsh winter, the only mail that can be delivered are letters.

One of my dogs had a litter of puppies. They are little balls of fur, with yipping barks and adventurous spirits. The one with a black circle around his eye will make a good sled dog, because he enjoys playing in the snow. I have sketched him for you. I am calling him Jack.

Mariah unfolded the other piece of stationery. A smile touched her lips at the ink line drawing of a playful-looking puppy.

Her gaze fell to the end and she read his signature.

Your loving father.

John James had studied the book filled with detailed drawings so intently that more than once she'd had to remind him steam engines weren't his schoolwork.

The next letter told of a winter storm and carried an update on the puppies. The following spoke of salmon fishing in icy rivers and camping with a native band of Cree fur traders.

What child wouldn't be delighted by these newsy letters and exciting accounts of sled races and gold strikes? Who wouldn't want someone always thinking of him? Who wouldn't feel important because someone with such an exciting life was sending all these newsy captivating letters? She herself admitted a deep-down fascination. Though skeptical of this man's motivation, she couldn't fault his attention to detail or the caring manner in which he addressed her child. The thing that disturbed her most was that closing at the end of each missive: *Your loving father.*

As much as she'd considered and reconsidered holding back the letter that told John James about this man's arrival, she'd told Grandfather to give it to him, and she'd only had to help him read a few of the words. Maybe Burrows wouldn't show up and she'd be spared, but John James would be heartbroken. She was pretty sure he'd turn up, though.

She believed he meant what he said, but there was no way of preparing. What did Wesley Burrows have to gain by perpetuating this charade?

She would know soon enough. She would know sooner than she'd like. However long it took him to get from Juneau City to Colorado wasn't long enough for her.

*Early June, 1882*

John James had been in a constant state of frenzied anticipation for the past week. He'd told everyone who would listen that his father was coming home. Every time Mariah heard him speak the words, another layer of rigid steel reinforced the protective shell around her heart.

"My father's coming home," he had proudly told the postman at the window in the Ruby Creek mercantile that afternoon.

Mariah had steadied her nerves and turned a page in the Montgomery Ward catalog. "Come look at these coats, John James," she said. "You need a new one."

"Your husband is returning?" Delia Renlow moved from where she'd been stroking a bolt of deep blue velvet to approach Mariah. "This is interesting news I haven't heard."

Dressed in a flowing green skirt and lacy shirtwaist, the curvy redhead dropped her gaze to Mariah's brown tweed trousers and scuffed boots.

Mariah managed a stiff smile. She'd attended school with Delia, but they'd never been friends. In fact Lucas Renlow, the man that Delia married, had once been sweet on Mariah. "Yes, Mr. Burrows will be here any day now."

"My goodness! Why how long has it been? You and your man will have to get acquainted all over again."

"He writes often," Mariah blurted, and then caught herself sounding defensive.

"A letter is no substitute for a flesh and blood partner,

now is it? How long has it been?" she asked again. She looked at John James. "Six years? Seven? I'd be surprised if you even remember what your husband looks like."

"Yes, well, we'd better be going. We're celebrating Grandfather's birthday this evening." Mariah hurried John James toward the door.

"Give my best to your granddaddy."

The brass bell attached to the door rang as Mariah escaped onto the boardwalk. The late-afternoon sun cast long shadows from the two-story wood frame buildings onto the hard-packed dirt street. In the distance a locomotive whistled, a sound she rarely noticed, but had been keenly attuned to the past several days. Would he arrive by train? Horseback? Wagon? She had no idea. She had studied the world map in John James's geography book to surmise that this Burrows fellow would take a steamship to the western coast of the United States. Train would be the quickest mode from there.

"Mama, you didn't order my coat."

"We have plenty of time," she assured him and took his hand and urged him toward the buggy she'd left several feet away.

That evening, the festivities commenced before dinner as family members arrived with platters of food. Wilhelm and Arlen had settled a keg of beer into the scrolled wrought-iron stand that had been in Grandfather's family for a hundred years. It now stood in the great room near the doorway where a hall led back to the kitchen and dining hall. A bucket sat below the spigot to catch drips, and Louis's two mountain hounds lapped at the overflow.

Mariah's grandmother had been gone nearly a decade, so as the oldest of their daughters, Mariah's mother supervised meals and holidays. Her blindness had no effect, since the family had carried out the same plans in the same manner for so many years that everyone knew their role. But Henrietta took her position seriously and reigned from her stool just inside the kitchen door.

"Where is the *rotkohl?*" her mother asked. "The dish hasn't gone to the table yet."

Mariah used flour sacks to pick up the steaming hot bowl of braised red cabbage. "Right here, Mama."

She and Faye exchanged an amused glance. Nothing passed without being detected by Henrietta's exquisite sense of smell.

Faye carried out egg noodles with mushroom sauce and Hildy followed with potato dumplings. The women had been cooking since the day before, and the house had remained filled with the mouthwatering aromas.

Mariah hadn't had much of an appetite recently, but tonight she was famished. She couldn't wait for her mother to give the word to begin.

Families grouped together, and the crowd became unusually quiet.

"Good health to the Spanglers!" her mother shouted.

A rousing cheer went up. Mothers helped their children prepare plates first. The youngsters sat at the long table in the kitchen, and the adults were welcome to prepare plates and eat in either the dining hall or the great room.

Mariah settled John James between Paul and Wilhem's boy August before going back for a plate for herself.

The line had already grown long, so she waited her turn beside Wilhelm and his wife, Mary Violet.

"How old is your grandfather?" Mary Violet asked.

Mariah and Wilhelm exchanged a glance. "Seventy this year?" Wilhelm asked and Mariah nodded.

At last Mariah filled her plate and took a seat in the great room. The room buzzed with conversation and laughter. One of Grandfather's dogs belched and flopped down beside his master's chair, raising a round of amused chuckles.

The door chimes rang, and Mariah distractedly noticed Marc rise and leave the room in the direction of the front hall.

A few moments later, the noise level dropped until the only sounds were forks settling on plates and voices from the dining hall.

Marc appeared in the doorway, a stranger beside him.

The few bites Mariah had eaten turned to stones in her belly. She paused with her fork in the air and stared.

The tall broad-shouldered man beside her cousin wore a brown straight-cut wool jacket over a red flannel vest, double-breasted shirt and black wool trousers. The outsider held a felt hat by the brim until Marc took it, along with his jacket and led the man farther into the room.

"She's right over there, Mr. Burrows."

Mariah froze in a moment of pure terror. A sound like rushing water filled her ears.

He was here.

# *Chapter Three*

The stranger's skin was deeply tanned except for feathered lines at the corners of his rich brown eyes, making him look as though he'd squinted against the sun for a lifetime. His russet-colored hair had been neatly cropped and was combed in waves against his scalp. One obstinate curl drooped at his temple.

He searched the faces of the people in the room with surprising intensity.

He wouldn't know her. The man everyone believed was her husband had never before set eyes on her.

Quickly handing her plate to Mary Violet, Mariah stood. She only wore skirts to church and for special occasions, and while a dress always made her feel naked and awkward, she felt even more vulnerable now. She brushed her damp palms against the fabric.

She'd drawn his attention, and he directed his dark gaze to her.

She took a few steps forward, then halted. Under the starchy skirts and petticoats, her knees shook.

He was taller than most of her brothers, but not as burly. He had a smooth, handsome forehead, a nice nose and well-defined lips. God help her, her gaze was drawn directly to a deep divot in the upper one.

Taking a few hesitant steps closer, she noticed the sweep of his dark brows and the shape of his square jaw. Just because his appearance took her breath away was no reason to weaken her resolve. This was the scoundrel who was up to no good.

His gaze never wavered from hers. "Mariah," he said.

Her first breath didn't produce anything, and it was a good thing, because she'd been about to blurt, *Mr. Burrows,* in front of her entire family. Instead she corrected her thinking and managed, "Hello, Wesley."

Louis straightened from his chair and made his way to where she and the unfamiliar guest stood gaping at one another.

"Welcome to Colorado, young Wes." Grandfather extended a hand. "Welcome to our home. It's a pleasure to meet you at last."

The stranger averted his gaze to the gentleman and shook his hand. "Thank you, sir."

Grandfather's mountain hounds sniffed at the stranger's boots and pant legs. He leaned forward and lowered a hand with his fingers curled under to let them learn his scent. After careful evaluation, one of the dogs licked him, and Wes turned his palm over to scratch its ear.

A few voices picked up conversations behind her, and others greeted Wesley with curious hellos.

The news had traveled as far as the kitchen, and Mariah knew the moment John James appeared in the great room. The expectant silence was deafening. Of course the irritating man had picked this night and this hour, and now her predicament was destined to play out in front of the entire Spangler clan. Mariah's heart hammered in apprehension.

All of her fears combined into a wave of dread, and she wanted to grab her boy and run with him until they were far away and safe, someplace where nothing could ever hurt him. But she couldn't. She was doomed to watch this unfold and deal with the consequences.

John James walked forward to stand beside her and curl his slender fingers into hers in the hidden folds of her skirt. He was afraid, too, but he was trying to be brave and not let on.

Wesley Burrows hunkered down until he was level with her child. The look in his obsidian eyes confused her even more. The look was almost relieved, almost desperate, almost…loving.

"John James?" he asked.

John James nodded, looked up at Mariah and then back. "Are you my papa?"

Mariah's throat grew tight with panicky denial. Denial she couldn't voice. Dozens of eyes were on them. She'd never fainted in her life, and she wasn't going to start now.

"I'm Wes Burrows," the man said. "I have all your letters. Every one. I've read them a hundred times."

"A hundred?"

"Maybe more."

John James's face lit with pure elation. "I read the book you sent. Mama helped me with the big words. There was lots of 'em."

The man glanced up at her with a crooked smile, but she averted her gaze to John James. As soon as they picked up their conversation, she studied him again.

His voice was deep and low, with a smoother accent than she was accustomed to hearing. "You're taller than I expected," Wes said.

"So are you."

The stranger smiled.

"Mama says I grow like a weed."

Mariah looked away so she wouldn't meet his eyes again.

"Did you cross the ocean?" John James asked with rapt fascination.

"I did. I had a stateroom aboard the *White Star* and came ashore in Seattle."

"I studied the ocean in my geography book," John James said with wide-eyed amazement. "Some ships sink in the water."

"Tragically, some do," he agreed.

Mariah had been unaware of her son's concern about this man's ship being lost, but putting herself in his place, he'd been without a father his entire life.

When he'd learned his was on the way, he'd likely imagined all manner of heartbreaking possibilities. She'd caused him this worry, but she'd had no choice. No choice in any of it.

John James's face was lit with discovery and pride. He turned to glance at the nearest family members.

For the first time, Mariah noted that Wilhelm and Arlen, along with her two older brothers, Gerd and Dutch, stood in a protective semicircle behind her and John James. Her gaze touched on each of their faces, noting their solemn expressions of concern. No doubt her body language hadn't alleviated their instincts.

With deliberate purpose, she relaxed her facial muscles and her shoulders, garnering her gumption for what she knew she must do. "Wesley," she said in the most cordial tone she could muster.

Immediately he stood, giving her his nerve-racking attention. "Yes, ma'am."

She turned to include her brothers in their circle. "Meet my brothers, Gerd, Dutch, Arlen and Wilhelm."

Wes shook hands with the fair-haired men one at a time, each man weighing the measure of the other in those brief grasps.

"I brought you something," Wes said, turning back to John James.

John James's eyes lit in anticipation. "What is it?"

"Wait right here." Wes turned and headed back for the front door, giving Mariah her first notice of the way he favored one leg in an awkward gait. John

James looked up at her. He'd noticed, too. So had everyone else.

Within moments, the man returned, but now all attention was drawn from his limp to the wooly white-and-gray puppy he carried over his forearm.

John James yipped his own bark of excitement and darted forward.

Grandfather's mountain hounds were every bit as interested as John James, wagging their tails and sniffing the air.

"You brought me a puppy?" John James asked excitedly. "What's his name? Did he come on the boat with you? What does he eat?"

This time when Wesley knelt to place the dog on the floor, Mariah noticed the way he grimaced, realizing the position caused him pain. "He's meant to be your dog, so you'll do the naming," he replied. "And yes, he and Yuri were good company on the trip. They've eaten a lot of fish. And small animals mostly."

"This isn't Jack, the pup you drew for me."

"No, Jack stayed up north to pull sleds. He wouldn't have been happy here."

The puppy was good-sized already, with unusual pale blue eyes and an erect head. It had a broad face and triangular ears, a bulky muzzle and a thick coat. Its facial markings looked like a white mask on his gray fur. Mariah had never seen a breed like it before. She knew from the letters that the puppy had been born to one of his sled dogs.

"Who's Yuri?" John James asked.

"Yuri's my dog," Wesley replied. "I sold all my others, but couldn't bear to part with him."

"Where is he?"

"Outdoors."

The young dog and the hounds sniffed each other with tails wagging.

Wes's charming grin turned up the corner of his lips. "Your pup's used to being around a pack of sled dogs and the rest of his litter."

John James reached for the puppy, and it backed away.

"Let him smell you first," Wes instructed. "Show him the back of your hand."

The furry dog sniffed John James's hand, licked it and then stood with his paws on John James's shirtfront.

The crowd murmured their appreciation and John James turned his face aside to avoid the dog's lapping tongue. He giggled with delight.

"You must be hungry." Henrietta had joined them and now stood just behind Mariah's shoulder.

Mariah turned and offered her mother her forearm. "This is my mother." Friederick joined them. "And my father."

Henrietta released Mariah to walk straight to Wesley. She raised her hand to his chest, then his shoulder. "You're tall."

Wes stood silent beneath her appraisal.

Henrietta raised both hands and ran them over his dark wavy hair, loosening another curl in the process, and then trailed her fingers over his forehead and nose.

"Isn't he a handsome one, Mariah?" she asked.

Mariah's neck warmed and the heat spread to her cheeks. Wes Burrows was definitely a ruggedly handsome man. The last thing she wanted to do was tell him she thought so, but she had to answer her mother. "He's a handsome one, Mama."

# *Chapter Four*

Laughter erupted around them.

Henrietta took Wesley's hand and placed it on her arm. "Come, get a plate and eat. It's my father's birthday and we're celebrating with our traditional dishes. Do you like *schweinswurst?*"

"I don't know that I've ever had it, ma'am. But the food sure smells good."

Mariah stood rooted in place as conversation swelled to normal. Her brothers blended back into the gathering, and her mother led Wesley toward the food tables.

Roth poured a mug full from the barrel and handed it to Wesley, who accepted the beer with a nod of thanks.

John James followed with the puppy at his heels and fed the animal bites of sausage without anyone scolding him.

Mariah's newly married sister, Annika, took

Mariah's hand and led her toward the dining hall. "This is an exciting day."

Mariah nodded.

"John James looks so happy."

Now Wes was seated at the long table and Henrietta directed Mariah's youngest sister Sylvia to fill his mug already. A heaping plate of food befitting a logger sat before him, and in between answering questions from others at the table, he seemed to be enjoying it.

Annika urged Mariah toward the empty chair beside him, and reluctantly, she took it.

"Where did you leave your plate?" Annika asked.

Mariah couldn't remember, so Sylvia brought her new servings and a fresh mug of beer.

Wesley glanced from the mug placed before Mariah to all the others around the table. The Spanglers drank beer with their meal as though it was water. Even the children had brimming mugs. He'd never seen beer served outside a saloon.

The food was pure heaven on his tongue, rich sauces and savory spices. This was a meal cooked by women who knew their craft and employed it seriously. His meals over a typical season consisted of salmon and small game roasted over an open fire. An occasional stay in a town sometimes garnered him a few vegetables and maybe a dried fruit pie that cost an arm and a leg.

"What is this?" he asked, of a particularly tasty serving on his plate and Mariah politely explained the potato dumpling.

She pushed around the food on her plate with her fork. It was plain she was uncomfortable with his presence, and he didn't really blame her. John James waited until a chair became available across from them and climbed up.

"Would you like some more to eat?" Mariah asked her son.

The boy shook his head and his gaze fixed on Wes.

The way the child looked at him made Wes sit a little straighter, eat his food a little more slowly. Clearly, the boy was completely enamored with having a father of his own.

A tiny arrow of guilt tried to stab his conscience, but Wes used his determination as a defense. He was giving John James the father he had longed for. He knew first-hand what it was like to see other kids with parents and have none. Of course, John James had his mother, a woman with fire in her eyes when she looked at him, though she avoided that most of the time.

She was spittin' mad.

Wes finished his meal and polished off another mug of beer. It was fine brew indeed, with a dark full flavor like nothing he'd enjoyed before. "I believe this is the best beer I've ever had."

Mariah nodded in her suspicious way, her wide blue gaze not lifting all the way to his. "Spangler Brewery makes the finest lager in the country."

"The children drink it, too," he remarked.

Something more flashed in her gaze when she directed it to him that time. Had he made her feel defensive? He hadn't meant to. "Some outside our culture find it an outrageous custom," she replied. "But we don't know anything different."

She had lustrous fair hair fastened in a loose knot atop her head, and skin as pale and smooth as the Chinese women who worked the laundries in the gold camps. Each time she looked at him, a rosy-pink hue tinted her complexion.

She was angry. Angry and wary, and he couldn't blame her. He wasn't even positive why he needed to make this trip and insert himself as John James's father, but he'd been pulled.

And after seeing the expression on the boy's face, after meeting him, he wasn't sorry. Not a damned bit sorry.

"Can I see Yuri?" the boy asked.

"Sure." Wes glanced aside at the boy's mother. "As long as your mama approves, we'll go outdoors later."

"How many dogs did you have?"

"Eight fine sled dogs," he replied. "Plus the occasional pups."

"Where did they sleep?"

"They camped under the stars with me," he replied. "Most usually I set up my tent and we all shared it. Keeps the snow from drifting over us during the night."

"You sleep right out in the snow with no house or nothing?"

"No houses out in the Yukon wilderness between towns and tent camps," he replied.

Two more children sidled in beside John James to listen. A girl and a smaller boy. "What did you eat?"

"These is my cousins, Emma and Paul," John James told him. "This here's my papa." The pride in his voice tugged at Wes's heart. "He delivers mail in Alaska." He turned back to Wes. "What did you eat?"

"Pleased to meet you," Wes said to the wide-eyed children, then replied to John James's question. "Sometimes I cut a hole in the ice and caught salmon for our suppers. Ate a lot of dried fish and dried meat during the day. In fair weather I found duck eggs and snared rabbits."

"Wasn't you scared of coyotes and mountain lions?" John James asked.

"No mountain lions, but I was always on the lookout for wolves and bears."

"Did you ever shoot a bear?" Paul asked.

"Yup. One time I had a good shot on an elk. Was looking down the barrel of my rifle when I heard branches snapping behind me. The elk bounded off." He gestured with a rapid swing of his arm. "I turned around to see a silver-tipped grizzly heading straight for me. That bear must've been twice as tall as me. At least he looked it from where I stood."

"What did you do?" one of the boys asked.

A few more children had joined them and now the adults had turned their attention to his story. One of Mariah's male cousins leaned against a doorway. Others stood nearby listening as attentively as the youngsters.

"I quick ran behind a tree and kind of circled it to buy some time. The bear followed and swiped at me. I didn't know how well I'd do shooting at it up close like that, but I fired. First shot didn't faze him."

"He didn't die?" John James asked.

"Nope, he raised up on his hind legs and charged forward. So I shot again. Must've hit an artery that time, 'cause blood spurted on the snow. That big fella lowered to all fours and took off running. About twenty yards down the hill, he fell over a log and died."

"What did your dogs do all that time?" Mariah's oldest brother Dutch asked from the corner, where he stood with a mug of beer.

"They're taught to stay quiet and wait for commands," Wes told him. "Protecting sled dogs can mean your life, and that load was my livelihood."

"What'd you do with the bear?" John James asked.

"Traded his hide for coffee and milk."

"You *skinned* 'im?" Paul asked.

"Ewww." Emma wrinkled her nose. "Grandfather has a bearskin in his room. It's icky."

"In the Yukon people use bearskins for blankets and rugs and even coverings for doorways," Wes explained. "The grease from their fat is used for all kinds of things."

"Let Mr. Burrows get comfortable now." Henrietta shooed away children and instructed her niece to remove his plate. "Come, Wesley. We'll sit by the fire. "Hildy will bring you some dessert."

"I'd better wait on the dessert, ma'am. I'm about to pop as it is."

"We gotta go see the other dog," John James reminded him.

Wes glanced at Mariah. "With your mother's permission."

She nodded her approval.

Henrietta rolled up a newspaper the women had scraped plates into, and handed it to him. Wes thanked her.

John James patted his leg to get the pup's attention, and the three of them headed out of doors.

Yuri met them with his tail wagging, but he didn't jump up or sniff at John James or the food until Wes gave him permission with a clicking sound.

"What did that noise mean?" John James asked.

"I told him he could come close and sniff. He won't jump on you. It's important for a work dog to be obedient, and it's especially important for a dog that's so strong."

It was obvious that the furry animal intimidated John James, and Wes understood that dogs of this breed were uncommon outside the far northern territories.

"Where is he gonna sleep?" the boy asked.

"He's used to being out-of-doors in all kinds of weather," Wes replied. "This is the fairest night he's ever seen. He'll sleep out here."

"Where is my puppy gonna sleep?"

"He's used to being outdoors, too. Pack dogs sleep close together to keep each other warm, and they get used to the company." Yuri had sniffed out the food, so

Wes opened the paper on the ground for him. "But honestly, that pup was a good bunkmate on the ship. So it's up to you to teach him where you want him to sleep."

"I'm gonna ask Mama if he can sleep with me. Grandfather's hounds sleep in his rooms with him."

Wes nodded. "All right."

John James looked at Yuri's harness. "Are you gonna tie him up?"

"Safer for him if he's loose."

"He won't run away?"

"He'll likely discover the woods yonder, but he'll come back."

Back inside, the blind woman greeted them and led Wes to the great room where, with a few words, she made seating space, then pointed for Mariah to sit on his other side.

John James settled on the rug with the puppy gnawing on a rubber ball beside him.

"Mama, can my dog sleep with me?"

Mariah observed the way her son stroked the animal's fur. "We'll give it a test to see if he does all right. You will have to learn to take him out before bedtime and again first thing in the morning. If there are any messes on your floor, he can't be your roommate."

"I promise," he said with all seriousness and gave Wes a pleased grin.

"Tell us of the women in Alaska," Henrietta prompted.

"Well, ma'am, the females are mostly from native

tribes, the Tlingits, Haidas, and Tsimshians…and near the coasts the Eskimos."

Little Emma had wedged her way into the gathering of children that had once again formed. "What do the Eskimos wear?"

"Sealskin leggings and coats, rabbit skin boots mostly," he replied.

"It sounds like a fascinating place," Henrietta commented.

"And beautiful in its own way. The cities are filled with sightseers," he told her. "They are the ones who pay the highest prices for food and mail delivery."

His gaze fell upon Mariah, seated quietly beside him, her slender fingers linked in her lap. She asked no questions, didn't even appear to be interested in the conversation, though she paid close attention to her son's animated face as well as those of her family members.

Faye brought Wes a cup of rich black coffee that smelled wonderful and tasted even better.

"Be off now," Henrietta told the children. "Give our guest air."

They obediently scrambled away.

He searched the faces of the family members, watched them interact with each other.

The children divided into groups to play games, and the adults picked up their own conversations.

Wes found it hard to imagine that John James and Mariah were related to every person in this room. Mariah had four brothers and two sisters he'd met so far, as well as an army of cousins, aunts and uncles, nieces and nephews.

He didn't know what it felt like to belong to a family. Or what it was like to look into a mother's face or see a father's hands and recognize where some part of him originated. What did it feel like to know the love and secure acceptance of people with the same name or the same eyes and a shared history?

He glanced around to make sure no one was listening and asked quietly, "You work at the brewery?"

Seeming startled that he'd addressed her directly, she nodded.

"What do you do?"

She, too, checked to see that no one overheard. "I oversee production and handle promotional events. Right now we're getting ready for the Exposition that opens in Denver July 17."

"I've heard talk of it. I read in the *New York Times* about the mining companies creating exhibits. Railroads and artists will have displays, too. They're going to start a two hundred and fifty horsepower Corliss engine on opening day. I read that the Denver hotels are booked already."

He'd been reading newspapers for the past couple of months, first while recuperating and then aboard the ship. Her surprised expression said she hadn't expected him to know so much about it.

"Over a year ago, I reserved an entire floor of rooms at a hotel. We've constructed a building inside the grounds where we'll cook, store lager and have displays of the brewery's history. An outdoor beer garden will be set up for entertaining."

"Sounds like an enormous undertaking."

"We'll be giving away beer the whole time. We have special bottles and labels. Handling the advance production has been a yearlong project. Some of us will be on site at all times, soliciting contracts. Now that we're bottling, this is an opportunity to spread our product and our name across the country."

It was more than she'd said since he'd arrived, and her enthusiasm for her subject was apparent. "Making beer is an unusual occupation for a woman."

"Not for a Spangler woman," she replied. "My mother and grandmother worked at the brewery. It's a *family* business."

He tilted his head. "I admire that."

She lifted her bright gaze and searched his face as though seeking his sincerity. She was lovely, this prickly woman, but her blue eyes sparked fire.

Her resentment was understandable. He was butting into her family. And because she had a secret she didn't want revealed, she wasn't calling him on his deceit. He wouldn't let himself feel bad about that. He was giving her son more than he was taking from her.

John James giggled and pulled his pant leg away from the puppy's nipping teeth, and Mariah turned her attention. Her entire expression softened when she looked at him.

Louis spoke to Wes about his friend Otto, whom Wes had known over the years he delivered mail from the Juneau City station, so they shared the loss of a friend.

Eventually the children grew tired and sought out their parents, and a trio of women came to stand before Wes and Mariah.

"We prepared your room," the one named Annika said. She was the same height as Mariah, but with much paler hair and a sprinkling of freckles. "Would you like me to help John James get ready for bed?"

Mariah stood quickly. "No, I can do it."

John James looked up at Wes with a hopeful expression. "Will you tuck me in?"

Wes glanced from his cherubic face to Mariah's barely disguised scowl. She gave a stiff nod that must have pained her.

"I will," he replied.

"Give us ten minutes," she said and took the boy's hand. "Annika, please show Wesley the way."

Her sister perched in the spot Mariah had vacated. "We've all been eager to meet Mariah's husband. John James has been talking about your arrival for weeks."

Wes smiled politely. "Pleasure to meet you, too, ma'am."

"Did you find any gold?"

"A little here and there. I settled on a job that was as good as gold, and a sure thing."

"As long as you survived the bears," Dutch added from across the room.

"There was that," Wes answered, and several of them laughed.

"Don't crowd the man," Louis said good-naturedly.

Eventually Annika got up to lead Wes through the foyer and up a wide set of curved stairs that opened into a comfortable open area with sofas, desks and shelves full of games and books.

"This is where the youngsters who live in the big house play and do their schoolwork," she explained. "John James's room is on the left down this hall." She stopped and indicated an open door.

Wes thanked her with a nod and entered.

John James lay in a narrow bed with a thick flannel quilt folded down to the bottom. On the other side of the room, a sleepy-eyed Paul watched them from a similar bed.

Mariah, who'd been sitting beside her boy, stood and backed away from John James's side, so Wes could approach.

"Hey, big fella," Wes said to her son.

"Hey. How come you walk like that anyway?"

"Got my leg stuck in a bear trap last winter," Wes told him. "It's all but healed now."

"I'm glad you're here," John James told him, his eyes solemn.

Wes's chest got tight. "I'm glad, too."

"I dreamed about you a hundred times."

"You did?"

"Uh-huh. An' you look just like I dreamed."

"Did I walk like this in your dreams?"

"Don't matter none to me."

Uncertainty overcame Wes in a torrent. This was why he was here. This boy needed a father. But how would he know what to do? How would he show John James love and teach him all he needed to know to grow up to be confident and proud? He didn't even know how to tell a child good-night. "Sleep well," he said.

A moment of silence passed.

"Papa?"

He wouldn't feel bad. He wouldn't. "Yes?"

"Mama says I'm not too big for hugs."

Wes's throat constricted. This impressionable, fragile little person believed Wes was the father he'd been yearning for. Wes had set himself up for an unbelievably huge responsibility. It didn't matter he'd never been on either end of a night like this. It didn't matter he couldn't find words. It didn't matter where he'd come from or that he had no previous examples of fatherhood or family. All that mattered was making a difference in this child's life…a difference for the better.

He perched on the edge of the bed. The instant he leaned forward, John James's skinny arms shot out and closed around his neck.

The little boy smelled like clean sheets and castile soap. His hair was cool and soft against Wes's cheek.

A hundred nights gazing at the aurora borealis couldn't compare to the wonder of a child in his arms.

Wes had come home.

* * *

Behind her, her sisters and cousin sniffled, and Mariah turned to see them dabbing tears from their cheeks. She had tears in her eyes, too, but they were from biting her tongue so she wouldn't scream at the intruder to clear the hell out of her son's room and leave their home.

"Go to sleep now," she said to John James.

"Papa, can you ride with me to school in the morning?"

Wesley tucked the covers around the boy's shoulders. "I suppose that'd be okay."

Mariah turned and headed out. Tucking in her son, walking him to school, letting her boy call him *Papa!* What was next?

Her sisters and Faye joined a row forming in the hallway. As she stepped into the hall, Mariah came face-to-face with the half dozen young women, all wearing expectant grins.

They appeared suspiciously happy about something, and she didn't like it one bit.

"Your room is ready," Faye said and took Wes's arm to lead him forward to the opposite door.

*Hold on, you're taking him to my room!* Mariah thought in a panic.

Sylvia caught her hand and smiled into her face. "Mariah's coming with us for a few minutes, Wes."

As the youngest and still unmarried sister, Sylvia had a room of her own at the end of the hall near their parents.

She and Annika swept Mariah into the confines of that room and guided her behind the dressing screen where a pitcher of warm water, towels and fragrant soap awaited.

"What do you think you're doing?" Mariah asked.

"Quickly now," Annika said. "Don't keep him waiting."

"What is this all about?" she asked.

Annika didn't wait, but came right behind the screen and turned Mariah away to unbutton her dress and push it to her hips. "We didn't get to do all this when you were first married because you were in Chicago. So we're doing it now."

Faye spoke from the other side of the screen. "It's easy enough to see that things are a little awkward between you two. We just want to give you a nudge in the right direction."

"It's natural to be nervous," Annika told her. "Your husband's been gone so long. But this is an exciting time, Mariah. Try to relax and enjoy his return."

Annika wet a cloth and soaped it. Mariah took it from her and shooed both of her sisters to the other side of the screen. "None of this is necessary."

They weren't listening to her. Even her cousins had filed into the room, and now stood giggling and teasing. Trapped in her web of deception, Mariah washed and dried, then yelped when Sylvia spritzed her with cologne. Both her sisters dropped a voluminous silky sheer nightdress over her head and tied the ribbons.

Mariah looked down in mortification. "You can see right through this!"

Faye laughed. "That's the idea!"

"Where did this come from?" Mariah asked.

"It's a gift from us." Annika tugged her forward and urged her to sit at Sylvia's dressing table. Mariah crossed her hands over her breasts in embarrassment. "I need my wrapper."

"You can't wear that old thing tonight," Annika told her.

In minutes, her hair was brushed, her cheeks powdered and Annika applied glycerin to her lips. Faye dropped a floral-patterned satin robe around her shoulders and Mariah gladly grabbed it and closed it around her.

They guided her along the hallway with the utmost giggling and shushing, finally pausing before her closed door.

"We're so happy for you, Mariah," Annika said in a throaty whisper. "Now get reacquainted with your husband."

One of them rapped and opened the door. Several pairs of hands urged Mariah through the opening. At the very last second, the robe was lifted away and out.

Mariah stood inside her closed door wearing only the sheer nightdress and a look of horror.

# Chapter Five

An oil lamp glowed from the top of a bureau, and a welcoming fire burned in a brick fireplace. The four-poster bed had been turned down and pillows with white cotton cases piled and fluffed for comfort. Wes stood studying the room, pondering his predicament. The Spangler women believed he was Mariah's husband… and as Mariah's husband, he would naturally be expected to sleep in this room with her.

His gaze traveled again to the bed. *Sleep with her.* Requesting another room or heading for the stables would drag up uncomfortable questions.

Behind him the door opened. He turned at the same moment someone entered, a flash of fabric whisked outward, and the door closed with a firm click.

Six mugs of beer had gone to his head, because he could have sworn a naked woman had joined him in this room. His mouth was suddenly so dry he wished he had another drink.

He should have turned away immediately, but not looking was impossible. She was real. Wes took in every lush curve and interesting hollow visible through the sheer white garment. He was a red-blooded, more-than-able-bodied man after all. And Mariah was incredibly beautiful.

She'd been frozen to the spot, but once she got her bearings and moved, she shot toward the bed, grabbed the coverlet and wrapped it around herself. It was too late. He had that creamy-skinned hourglass body and those lush dusky-tipped breasts seared on his brain for eternity. To what fortuitous hand of fate did he owe the privilege of meeting her son and seeing her naked all in the same day?

"I will never forgive them for this. Never!" She gathered the folds of the bedcover and dragged it behind a bamboo dressing screen with her. "You might have looked away," she said from the other side.

"Might have," he agreed.

Only then did he hear the soft laughter and the hushed giggles coming from the hallway.

"A gentleman would have," she added.

"Might have," he said again.

The rustling sound of fabric told him she was putting something on, a nightdress perhaps. A real nightdress.

"Forget that happened," she begged.

*Not if I live to be a hundred.* He said nothing. His presence here was lie enough.

She came out from hiding wearing a printed cotton wrapper that covered her all the way from her throat to her ankles. She draped the coverlet over the bed before going straight to a small table with three hinged mirrors, where she grabbed up a hairbrush. She made a few brisk strokes through her lustrous mane of fair, wavy hair before sectioning it off and braiding it. Her cheeks were still crimson with embarrassment—or anger. Both probably.

"First," she said, coming to stand a safe few feet away from him. The thick braid fell over her shoulder and swayed against her breast. "I want to know what you're doing here."

"Didn't your grandfather share my letter?"

"You want my son to have a father," she stated.

"It's more than that. I don't know that I can explain it to you."

"Try." With her hands on her hips, she pursed her glistening lips and waited, her body held stiff. Her flowery, feminine scent played havoc with his restraint. He knew what was beneath that dressing gown.

He took a deep breath and exhaled. He deserved her suspicion, of course. She didn't know him. "Can we sit down? I've traveled a far piece on foot today."

Her accusing gaze faltered, and she frowned as though she regretted having to change her opinion of him from an ogre to a human being. "Yes, of course. Take the chair there by the fire."

With his ankle and calf throbbing, he made his way

over to the chair and sat. It took him a couple of minutes to get his boots and socks off.

She appeared to wrestle with herself for a moment, but then darted forward. "Will it help to raise it?" she asked. She dragged a small trunk within reach and placed a needlepoint pillow atop it. "Rest your foot."

"Thank you, ma'am." Though he didn't take a shine to showing his weakness, he had no choice but to use both hands to lift his leg and set his foot atop the pillow.

She leaned over to adjust the cushion, and her braid fell against his bare ankle. She straightened, glanced away and then back. "A bear trap?" she asked.

"Can't see 'em in the snow," he answered. "That's the idea, of course, but this one was set along a trail.

"Passed out a couple of times before I got the rusty contraption off. Used my first-aid supplies to clean and bandage it, but I lost a lot of blood. Would've died if a band of Haida hadn't found me. They doctored my leg and took me on to Juneau City 'cause they saw the mail bags."

"What's a Haida?"

"A native tribe that mostly hunts whales and fish along the coast, but some travel inland. Lucky for me these did. Anyway, infection traveled up my leg, and I was in a bad way for months."

Mariah perched on the foot of the bed, then curled her feet up under her wrapper to lean against one of the posts on the footboard as she listened.

"When I came around, the new station man said my box was full and brought me the stack. All letters from your boy," he said. "Letters addressed to me. I shared a room right there at the station when I was in the city, so that's where I spent the next few months, laid up and reading letters. Couldn't figure out why this young fella was writing to me like he knew me, like I was somebody special."

Mariah's gaze shifted to the hem of her sleeve and she smoothed a finger over it without speaking.

"It probably doesn't make much sense to you or to anybody…I'm kind of confused by it myself—but those letters were a connection for me. Something to hang on to. Something to look forward to and see me through another day. I searched old Otto's room and found the rest, along with several from Louis. Eventually I wrote back to your grandfather."

Mariah looked up and sighed. "And he told you it wouldn't hurt if you picked up where Otto left off."

"That's the gist of it, yes."

She shook her head. "I didn't disagree with him. I never did. I just let him create this whole fantasy and played right along with it because it was convenient."

Wes heard the concern in her voice. Her next words proved it.

"What are you going to do with this information now?"

He appreciated her freshly scrubbed face, shiny hair and pink lips. She was the prettiest woman he'd laid eyes on in a month of Sundays. "What do you mean, ma'am?"

"We used your name and your mailbox, and it was wrong of us. Have you told anyone?"

"No, of course not. I don't care that you used my mailbox. Or my name for that matter. As it turned out John James's letters might have saved my life." He'd been alone for so long, that those letters had been a life connection for him. "That probably sounds a little dramatic, but it's not much of an exaggeration."

"What do you want from him? From me?"

"I don't want anything, Mariah. I want to give something to him. I want to make a difference."

She slid her feet to the floor to stand again, and he noted they were slender and bare. *Like the rest of her beneath that plain cotton dressing gown.*

"What does that mean exactly?" she asked. "How do you plan to make a difference? How is playing out this lie going to do anything except make things worse?"

"How will I make it worse?"

"By disappointing him," she said hastily and then lowered her voice. "By lying to him."

"*You're* already lying to him. I'm making it real. I'm bringing him the father he wants."

She pressed her palm to her forehead and closed her eyes for a moment before raising her head to glare at him. "How dare you presume? You are not real. And you are not the father he wants. I don't even *know* you!" She caught herself raising her voice again and lowered it to say, "*He* doesn't know you."

"I'm here to fix that."

She stepped closer. "To what end, Mr. Burrows? How do you plan to step into the imaginary role of his father and not disappoint him? Someday he's going to learn the truth."

"How?"

She stared at him.

"How will he learn the truth? According to you, only three of us in the entire world know. Is that a fact?"

"It is."

"Nobody else?"

"No one."

"Do you think your grandfather will tell him?"

"Of course not."

"I haven't pried into your business, but now that you've brought it up, what *is* the truth? Is his real father going to show up?"

She looked away. "No."

"Then how will he find out? Do you plan to enlighten him when he's older?"

The lantern light picked up the sheen of tears in her eyes. "Why are you really here?" she asked. "What do you want from us?"

She blinked and turned her back to him, gripping the bedpost so tightly, her knuckles turned white.

It didn't matter how much his leg complained, Wes had to get up and go to her. Her feelings were justified. Her fears were real. He stood behind her, close enough to detect the trembling in her body. He reached out to place his hand on her shoulder and reassure her of his intent.

The moment his fingers touched her wrapper, she flinched and spun to face him, her eyes wide with mistrust.

"I didn't mean to frighten you."

She raised her chin a notch. "I'm not afraid of you."

She was a lovely creature, with skin as pale and satiny-looking as fresh cream. Her vivid blue eyes conveyed her wariness, wounding him unexplainably. He didn't want to hurt her or the boy. How could he make her understand?

He took a few steps back.

"You haven't thought this out," she said. "You want to be a part of my son's life, but what about me? What if I don't want you in my life?"

"Look, I know there's a lot to think about, a lot we have to talk about. But be honest. Don't you think it would be best for him to have a father?"

Her exasperation was plain in the way she opened her mouth but said nothing, as though she didn't even have a reply.

"You'll leave," she said finally, and he thought the words must have hurt the way she hesitated over them. "One day you'll tire of the charade and move on. And what will happen to him then?"

"I don't have any intention of leaving." His voice was soft, but filled with rigid determination. "Not now and not later. I've come to stay. For good."

Mariah wanted to throw something at him. The man was presumptuous and delusional and...*oh my goodness,* but he smelled incredible. Like a warm night breeze in the mountains.

There was no escaping the effect he had on her. When he lowered his voice and spoke so intently, goose bumps raised along her skin. He didn't have to touch her for her to know how disturbingly close he stood. From the beginning, she'd sensed every time he looked at her, knew the moment he moved closer. What was she going to do about him?

"What are you doing to us?" she asked, hating that a fat tear escaped her rigid composure and slid down her cheek.

"I understand that you don't trust me." He spoke so calmly that it angered her all the more. He was calm, rational…unless one actually listened to the foolish words he spouted. "You haven't had time to learn I can be trusted," he added.

"You're crazy." She scrambled away from him to the opposite side of the bed where she folded down the sheet.

"Do you want me to go somewhere else?"

She confronted him across the mattress. "Where? Where would you go that my family wouldn't see you and question why I'd kicked my newly returned husband from my room?"

"I don't know. I could—"

"No, you've butted your way in here and made everybody like you. Everyone thinks you're—you're—who you say you are."

"I am who I said I am. I'm Wes Burrows."

"But you're not my husband."

"I never said I was, ma'am. You did."

"Oh!" She picked up a pillow and threw it at him. He caught it easily. Then she bunched up the coverlet she'd held around her earlier and tossed it toward him. "Sleep on the window seat. Or the floor. I don't care where. I have to get up early in the morning."

"Should we compare stories?" he asked. "So I don't make any mistakes?"

She reached for the lamp that sat on a table at the side of the bed. "Be gone from this room by the time I wake in the morning." She turned down the wick, plunging the room into darkness. "When we're alone, you stay as far away from me as possible."

A satisfying thump like that of his knee or foot hitting wood was followed by a barely audible groan. She climbed into the bed and pulled the sheet up over her head.

This had been the worst night of her life.

That hasty thought unleashed a torrent of chilling memories—the night before Hildy's wedding, a night she tried never to think of. Tonight had been far from the worst night of her life. But it rated right up there.

She hugged her pillow, curled up in a ball and used every ounce of her grit not to wail like a baby. She had to keep her wits about her and her chin held high. Her troubles had only just begun.

Wes had slept in a lot worse places. A plush rug in a warm room with a snapping fire was no hardship compared to a smelly fishing ship being tossed on the sea or subzero winter nights in a tent. He woke at first light and crept from the house.

Yuri met him when he exited the back door. If the twigs in his fur were any indication, the dog had been hunting. Wes sat on the step to pet the animal and pick out sticks and leaves. Yuri licked his stubbled chin.

So maybe he hadn't thought this move all the way through. He'd considered the part about being a father to a fatherless boy, but he hadn't thought about being a husband to a woman who wanted no part of him.

After several minutes, Wes found a pump and basin in an outbuilding behind the house, where he washed and shaved.

He was just finishing up when Mariah's cousin Marc entered. He lit the old stove and set a kettle of water on top. "First one out starts a fire," Marc told him.

"Guess I forgot about hot water," Wes answered. "I was tickled there was no ice on top of the barrel. I'll remember tomorrow." Yuri, who'd waited outside the wash building, followed him back to the house.

"Breakfast isn't formal," Henrietta said from where she stood cutting and wrapping a mountain of sandwiches. "Food's set out on the sideboard in the dining room. Bring your dirty plate in here when you're finished."

"Thanks, ma'am."

Wes joined the Spanglers vying for a spot in line and prepared himself a plate. Enjoying this many hot meals in a row, meals that he hadn't searched for firewood to cook, was a treat.

"What will you do after you ride with me to school?" John James asked. He had saved a chair next to him at the table.

Wes had figured he could find a job in town, but if he was going to be living here, it seemed he should be working where all the family members worked. "I guess I'll be looking for a job."

John James chuckled. "You don't hafta look. There's lot of jobs at the brewery. Right, Mama?"

Wes glanced up to find Mariah holding a plate and a mug of coffee while she waited for one of the children to finish eating. Her attire drew his attention. She wore a brown pair of men's trousers that outlined the shape of her hips and thighs and cinched her narrow waist. Immediately the vision of her shapely limbs and ivory skin entered his thoughts. The sight of her nakedness would never stop taunting him.

"I don't do the hiring," she said as though relieved about the fact.

John James's cousin left and she slid onto a chair across from her son. She was as fresh and pretty as ever, with her skin glowing and her shiny hair knotted on top of her head. He couldn't help remembering the sight of the wavy tresses flowing across her shoulders, her breasts peeking through filmy fabric.

The ivory skin across her cheekbones took on a pink hue, as though she suspected where his thoughts had traveled.

"Who does the hiring?" Wes asked.

"My father," she replied. Was that a hint of pleasure he detected in her voice?

She had barely finished her eggs and toast when a bell rang from outside.

"That's the wagon headed for the brewery." She took a man's cap from her hip pocket and settled it over her hair at a jaunty angle. "Your books are beside the front door, John James."

"Bye, Mama." He hugged her, then turned to Wes. "We ride to school in the other wagon that's out front."

Wes joined the children, who were driven to school by Sylvia.

As they entered the small white schoolhouse, John James introduced him to each youngster they passed. "This is Wesley Burrows, my papa," he told them proudly.

"Miss Saxton, this is my papa," he told the woman greeting all the children.

The pleasant-faced woman offered her hand. "Pleased to meet you. I'm Margaret Saxton."

"Wes Burrows, miss."

"We've heard all about you. John James has been bursting with excitement, awaiting your arrival."

"I was pretty eager to get here, myself." He turned to John James. "Be on your best behavior today."

"Yes, sir." The boy beamed a smile as he waved goodbye.

Wes exited the schoolhouse and settled his hat on his head. Still on the seat of the wagon, holding the reins, Sylvia waited for him. "Want a ride to the brewery?"

"That where you're headed?"

"No, I do the shopping for Mama and help Hildy with laundry and chores. But it's easy enough to drop you off."

He climbed up. "Seems everybody in the family pretty much has their place, taking care of the house and running the brewery."

She flicked the reins over the horses' backs. "If you're wondering if you'll fit in, the answer is yes. We all want Mariah to be happy. And she needs her man around to be happy."

Being referred to as her man was almost uncomfortable, but on a deeper level, he liked it. He sat a little straighter on the hard seat. "I guess it seems odd to a family like this that...that she hasn't had her husband here all this time."

"I can't speak for everyone, but Mama and Annika and I don't hold it against you that you took off the way you did," she said. "You're here now."

"Everyone has been very kind."

"Everyone wants what's best for Mariah—and John James," she replied.

Wes's first glimpses of Spangler Brewery held three smokestacks billowing gray plumes into the sky. Drawing closer, he made out the perfectly flat land where several three- and four-story buildings sat in precise arrangement around a courtyard, with smaller buildings between. The tallest brick structure sported a cupola with a weather vane.

"That's where the offices are," Sylvia said, pointing

to the building he'd noticed. "Grandfather and Papa are in there."

She reined the horses to a halt. He thanked her and climbed down with his weight on his good ankle.

The enormous courtyard bustled with activity. Teams of horses pulled loaded wagons toward an open-sided building and four men stood in the shadow of a tall brick clock tower, holding a conversation that involved energetic hand waving. One man beat his hat against his thigh as he spoke.

Wes headed beneath the arched brick entryway, through a set of heavy doors and into a silent lobby.

# Chapter Six

A man in a three-piece suit greeted him.

"I'm here to see Friederick Spangler," Wes told him.

"I'll let him know you're here," the man said and proceeded down a long hallway, giving Wes too much time to wonder what Mariah had told her family about him—rather about her supposed real husband. He might as well plan some fancy dancing if subjects he couldn't answer came up. He and his "wife" needed to talk more than they had, but that was going to be a challenge.

"Are you Wesley Burrows?" the man called a few minutes later.

"I am."

"Go right in." He pointed to a door.

"I was expecting you." Instead of sitting behind a desk as Wes had expected, Mariah's father sat on an upholstered chair, a table holding stacks of paper beside him. "Have a seat."

Wes took a chair across from his. The older man had a narrow face bracketed by neat sideburns laced with gray. He wore trousers and a dun-colored work shirt. "You here for a job?"

"Yes, sir."

"Know anything about making lager?"

"That I don't."

"Drank your share?"

He grinned. "Is that a job requirement?"

Friederick laughed. "No. Just the remark I most often hear from townspeople who apply. Not everyone here is family." With his elbows on the arms of the chair, he laced his fingers and looked at Wes over his knuckles. "Plenty of us have wondered about you."

Wes gave him an understanding nod. "That's normal."

"Questioned more at first. It was hard to understand how a newly married man with a baby could leave them to fend for themselves while he sought his fortune."

Wes wasn't sure what to say. He had no idea how a man could do that, either.

"I know you sent her money," Friederick said. "Money wasn't what she needed. She and my grandson have always been well cared for. What she needed was a man at her side. A father for her boy."

"I know that, sir. That's what I intend to be. Now."

"Nothing to say for yourself?"

"What could a man say that would make up for that?" he asked. "I have to prove myself to her now. To

John James. To all of you. A man deserves a chance to do that, doesn't he?"

"You have six years to make up for," the man said. "That's a pretty big job."

"I believe I can do it, sir."

Friederick scrutinized him long and hard, taking measure…weighing. "I guess we'll see." He lowered his hands. "Don't hurt them."

"No, sir."

Friederick got up and walked to the window. "You realize that just because you're married to Mariah doesn't give you special rank here."

"I expect to earn my way. Always have."

"You have a lot of catching up to do in order to learn this business. Learning will take extra time and effort. You up to that?"

"I am."

"Can't help but notice you have a limp."

"My leg has healed. I can do a day's work like any man."

Friederick turned back to face him. "All right then. I'm sending you to the mash house. My nephew Philo is the superintendent of that building. You'll answer to him."

Preparing to leave, Wes stood. "Which building is the mash house?"

Philo Ulrich stood as tall as Wes, but was a whole lot broader across the chest and shoulders. Wes had noticed him at the party the evening before, but some of the family relationships were still confusing.

"You're gonna pull your weight just like every other man here," Philo yelled in front of a dozen men in the high-ceilinged building. Sweat plastered his reddish hair to his forehead. Steam engines, belts and pulleys were so loud that he had to shout to be heard. The smell, like sickly sweet oatmeal, was almost overpowering.

"Mr. Fuermann wants you to have a working knowledge of what goes on here, so today you're going to watch and learn about starch conversion. Tomorrow I'm starting you out on the heat tanks."

By Mr. Fuermann, he meant Friederick, Wes figured out, and listened as Philo spouted orders to each man. Wes noticed that though quite a few women were employed at the brewery, the workers in this particular building were all men. It didn't take long to figure out why. The work was hot and dirty and took a lot of muscle.

By lunchtime, Wes's head was ready to explode from the smells, the lengthy explanations of tanks and malt-mills. Grist cases and mashing machines shouted at him alongside steaming tanks and chugging engines. The conditions were chaotic to a man used to spending weeks at a time alone in the vast wilderness.

A whistle blew from the courtyard, and the men paused in their tasks. Machines went blessedly silent and conversations sprang up. Wes followed the workers across the courtyard to an open-sided building. The sandwiches Henrietta had wrapped were sitting out, along with metal tubs of apples and a cask of beer with a spigot.

As couples, families and friends sought out each other, he noticed that Philo paired off with Mariah's cousin Hildy to eat.

After picking up his food, Wes spotted Mariah and approached her hesitantly. She still wore her cap, and there were smears that looked like grease across the back of her trousers. He sure didn't mind the way she looked in those trousers. Did she have any idea of how she drew attention to one of her best features by wearing them?

She turned and met his appraisal. There was no way she could know what he was thinking, but she drew her brows together as though she had. Jerking her gaze to the onlookers, she motioned for him to join her at a table near the back.

A quick search of the room showed that most eyes were indeed upon them. With appreciation, he watched her seat herself and then sat across from her. His ankle had been aching for the last hour, so he propped it on the bench beside him and unwrapped his sandwich.

Mariah picked up her sandwich. "Where did he assign you?"

"The mash house. The smell takes some getting used to."

Her gaze flickered to his, then across the room,

where it settled briefly on Hildy and Philo before moving away.

"They're married, Hildy and Philo?" he asked.

She nodded. "The smell will change. During the boil, once the hop is added, the mash takes on a sweeter floral aroma."

He absorbed that information. "I thought Hildy stayed at the house with your mother."

"She brings lunch."

"I never knew there was so much that went into making beer."

"Bottom-fermented lagering is an art," she replied. "Grandfather is rather old for the brewmaster title, but my mother is his oldest child, and my oldest uncle was killed several years ago. The title rightfully belongs to my uncle Patrick, but he's happy to let Grandfather continue."

"The difference is obvious," he said, "from what I'm used to being served."

"About all that's sold throughout the upper states and Canada is ale or top-fermented lager," she told him. "We're working to infiltrate markets dominated by whiskey, cider and Americanized English ale. Now that we have machinery, we can produce faster and create a better product."

"Why better?"

"More uniform, I should have said." She drank from her mug. "This is a very good year for us," she continued.

"Why is that?"

"Last winter was warm. Made ice scarce and expensive for a lot of the major breweries that don't have ice-houses. We've been using ice machines for about eight years. The Exposition is the best opportunity we've ever had to present our product to the country."

For the second time, she'd been drawn into affable conversation because it involved the brewery, and Wes filed away the information. She reminded him of the enterprising women who lived and worked in Alaska. There weren't many, but those few who had started their own businesses were smart and capable, and some of them even wore trousers.

None he'd seen had ever looked as good in their trousers as Mariah did, however. The building seemed a lot warmer than it had when they'd entered.

The whistle blew again, and she rolled up the paper wrapping from her lunch and stood. "You done?"

He finished his beer, grateful for the cool liquid. "Thanks for sitting with me, ma'am."

She walked ahead of him and they threaded their way into one of the lines moving outside. "I didn't have any choice."

She cut away and headed for one of the other buildings.

Wes took a deep breath and walked toward the mash house.

The next few days followed pretty much the same pattern. He told John James goodbye at the front of the house and then hopped on the back of a wagon heading for the brewery. For ten hours—with a break for lunch—Philo tested Wes's mettle, and Wes determinedly worked to prove himself.

Of an evening, he sat beside John James and across from Mariah at the supper table, learning what it was like to be part of the chattering, laughing family that pulsed around him.

Mariah's mother often sought him out in the uncanny way she had about her. She would tilt her head and moments later, walk right up beside him.

One evening as they joined others by the fire, Henrietta laid her hand on his shoulder, and then took his hand. "Your husband is in pain," she told Mariah a few minutes later.

"I'm all right, Mrs. Fuermann."

"I can call the doctor for you," the woman told him.

He shrugged. "There's nothing he can do except give me something for the pain. My leg is healing on its own."

"Put ice on it," she told Mariah. "And then you heat a bag of rice. That will feel good and help him sleep. Have you been sleeping well?"

"Just fine, ma'am."

"I don't think so. I think you're tired." And to Mariah she said, "Take your husband upstairs now."

Mariah stood. "Head upstairs, John James."

Her son carefully piled his wooden horses in their canvas bag. "Come on, boy," he said unnecessarily to the dog he'd named Felix. The critter followed him everywhere.

She glanced at Wes. "You two go ahead. I'll be right up."

"Did you see my horse that looks like an army horse?" John James asked as they climbed the stairs.

Wes took each step with caution so as not to bend his ankle at a painful angle. "You'll have to show it to me up close," he replied.

With Felix at his heels, John James ran ahead into his mother's room. Wes followed more slowly. The child knelt on the rug and took his horses from the bag—right where Wes normally made his pallet for the night. Wes eased onto the plushly upholstered chair and listened as John James told him about each horse.

Minutes later, Mariah joined them, softly closing the door behind her. She glanced from her son to Wes and then at the bed. She set her mouth in a line of displeasure, but she set down the knotted dishtowel she held on the night table, pulled back the covers on the near side of the bed and propped several pillows. "Come lie down," she told him.

He took off his boots, then limped to the bed and made himself comfortable on the soft mattress.

She placed another pillow near the end and instructed him to rest his foot on it.

He did so, and she retrieved the dishtowel, which it turned out was filled with ice, and held it above his leg. She paused. "Where, exactly?"

Wes hiked up his pant leg and rolled down his wool stocking so she could see the scars.

"It's swollen," she said with surprise.

"Not bad."

She arranged the cold pack on his leg.

"Thank you, ma'am."

She avoided his gaze. "You don't have to call me ma'am."

"Tell us a story, Papa," John James begged, climbing onto the foot of the bed. "Please?"

Mariah reached into a small brocade satchel and took out some kind of stitchery, then sat on the rocking chair near the bed.

"Is that needlepoint?" Wes asked.

"Embroidery. I'm making a quilt for my cousin's baby."

"Hildy?" he asked. It took a lot of doing, but he was trying to remember names and relationships.

A frown lined her forehead for only a second before she said, "Hildy has no children. Faye is expecting a new one."

"A new brother or sister for Paul and Emma," he said, proud that he'd made the correct family connection.

The ice did feel good on his leg, and he was able to relax a little. He considered a story for John James. "One winter there was so much snow north of Skagway that it drifted twenty feet and more in some places up toward the Yukon. I wouldn't risk my dogs and neither would the other carriers, so we waited for a melt.

"The mail piled up so high that we had to build

frames for canvas tents and then guard the bags at night."

"Why did you have to guard a bunch o' letters?"

"Newspapers are more valuable than jewels to people hungry to hear what's going on in the world and want news from back home. And sometimes there's money in the letters. Dishonest people don't care who the mail is addressed to if they want it badly enough."

"Did Yuri help you guard the mail?"

"I pitched my tent nearby, and the dogs were tied beside it," he answered. "News came about one postmaster who couldn't take the stress of all the mail piling up and the unhappy customers. He set fire to the pile."

"Did all the mail burn?" John James asked.

"Nah. The citizens caught the postmaster, put out the fire and ran him out of town." His ankle was numb and aching from the cold. "Can I take this off now?"

Mariah got up and removed the ice pack. "I have the hot one warming," she said and left the room.

A few minutes later she returned with a bulging sock.

"That's rice?" he asked.

She placed it on his ankle. "Yes."

"It's sure hard."

She blinked and looked from him to his leg. "Well, it's not cooked."

"Oh."

She laughed then, a surprising burst of sound that made him feel foolish, but warmed him all the same.

"I had no idea," he said. "I've never heard of this."

"Your mother never gave you a sock filled with rice for a stomachache?" she asked.

"Never knew my mother," he replied.

Her expression turned solemn and she cast that skeptical blue gaze on him. "She died?"

"I don't know."

She returned to her chair and picked up her embroidery, but didn't look at it.

"I grew up in a foundling home," he told her.

John James's attention had been snagged. "What's a foundling home?"

"An orphanage," Mariah explained. "Where children with no parents are taken care of."

"But *everyone* has parents," John James said.

"Not all parents stick around," Wes told him. "And some die. Andrew Jackson was an orphan."

John James swung his worried blue gaze to his mother. "You won't die, will you, Mama?"

"Of course not, sweetling. Your mama's as healthy as one of your uncle Dutch's prize pigs."

John James laughed, which is what she must have intended. When his smile faded, he wrinkled his forehead and looked back at Wes. "But what about your grandmama or your aunts and uncles? Couldn't you have gone to live with them?"

Wes shrugged. "Guess there wasn't anyone. Nobody who wanted me anyhow."

"How long did you stay there, at the foundling home?" John James asked.

"I was apprenticed to a doctor in Ontario when I was about ten or so," Wes answered.

John James's eyes widened. "You're a *doctor?*"

Wes shook his head. "All I ever did was muck stalls and split wood. I ran off and worked a whaling ship."

John James got up and came to stand beside him. "Did you see whales?"

"Inside and out," he replied.

"Did one ever swallow you?"

"All right, enough questions," his mother said. "Pick up your horses and go get ready for bed."

"Yes, ma'am." John James hunkered down to gather his toys. "Jonah got swallowed by a whale. He's in Grandfather's Bible."

"I'll tell you about whaling another night," Wes promised.

John James set down the bag and walked up beside the bed. "You helped tuck me in all the other nights. I can tuck *you* in this time."

He climbed on the side of the bed to lean over and give Wes a hug. "Aren't you gonna take off your trousers and shirt?"

"In a bit. Good night, John James."

The boy pulled up the sheet and blanket over Wes's clothed form. "Good night, Papa."

He grabbed his bag, patted his thigh so Felix would follow and scurried from the room, Mariah close behind.

The warmth seeping from the hot rice into his leg had

relieved the ache. Wes hadn't felt so relaxed in a long time. He missed Yuri's company at night, but his own presence alone was enough imposition; he could hardly bring the dog in, as well. Besides, Yuri wasn't used to sleeping in warm temperatures.

Neither was he, Wes thought, but he was adjusting just fine.

He closed his eyes to rest in comfort a moment longer.

Felix settled down right beside John James, the dog's chin resting on its paws. The animal gave Mariah a beseeching blue-eyed stare, and she petted its furry head. Between Wes and this dog, she'd never seen John James so animated or content.

"It's sad Papa didn't have a family, isn't it?" John James asked, his lips turned downward in sympathy. "I never knew anybody what din't have a family."

Mariah had to agree that if that story was true, it was indeed sad that the man had grown up alone and unwanted. "A lot of people have to deal with things that aren't perfect in their lives," she told him. "He grew up just fine."

"But he doesn't have to be alone any again," he told her. "He has us now."

She smoothed his hair and kissed his forehead. "Indeed."

If his story had been intended to work on their sympathies, it had worked on John James. She would reserve her judgment about the sincerity of his youthful plight.

A minute later, Mariah closed John James's door. She slipped down the back stairs to dip a pitcher of water before returning to her own room. Or rather the room that should have been her own. How she'd ended up sharing it with a stranger was incomprehensible.

Wes's eyes were closed and his features relaxed in peaceful comfort. Setting down the pitcher on the washstand, she steeled herself against having sympathy for his pain. He shouldn't have been here in the first place. He'd horned his way into this house and into her family—and even her room—without any rights whatsoever.

His presence was a blackmail of sorts. He held her over a barrel because she couldn't deny him or discredit him without exposing her life as a monumental lie.

Looking at him lying in her bed, a quivering unease gripped her. She closed her eyes and took several deep breaths to fight off the panicky, trapped feeling.

Her life was a monumental lie.

As long as she never had to think about it—admit it—she scurried from day to day, handling the tasks that needed to be done, losing herself in caring for the son she loved beyond life itself, staying busy with work…

But coming face-to-face with the harsh truth— having this stranger encroach upon her privacy— knowing that he had discovered a small part of her lie and was using that knowledge for his own purpose… this was unbearable.

If it weren't for her child lying in bed across the hall,

she would pack a bag and run as far away as she could. Her hands were shaking and clammy when she raised them to her cheeks.

Mariah opened her eyes and looked at her trembling hands. She would *not* give him the power to do this to her.

She stomped behind the dressing screen and changed into her cotton nightdress, then washed and dried her face and hands. She unrolled the comforter and blanket he stored in the armoire each night and spread them on the floor. Her mother would heartily disapprove, but then her mother didn't know Mariah had never seen this man before he'd arrived a little over a week ago.

"Please move from my bed now," she said from a safe distance.

He didn't flicker an eyelash.

She took a step forward and poked his shoulder. "Please move from my bed now."

Still he remained unmoving.

She grabbed one of the pillows from beneath his head and batted him with it. "Get out!"

# Chapter Seven

She'd startled him, and Wes shot to a sitting position, instinctively snatching the pillow. Mariah didn't let go quickly enough, so the momentum jerked her toward him.

She fell across his lengthy form. Thankfully the pillow wedged between them, but she was too close. He clamped a hand on her upper arm to steady her. Instinctive panic fogged her vision and blocked rational thought. She clawed his hand away to escape his hold.

"What the hell, woman?"

Jerking from his grip and struggling to stand, she got to her feet and threw the pillow at his pallet. Out of breath, she backed away, and then pointed at the floor.

Warily eyeballing her, he ran a hand down his jaw, and swung his legs over the side of the bed. The sock with the rice fell upon the covers with a tiny swish.

She took another step away.

"You might've tried to wake me gentle-like."

"Might have," she said, mocking what he'd said to her about looking away the night her sisters and cousins had shoved her in the door nearly naked.

He cast his penetrating dark gaze her way.

A minute passed during which she speculated whether or not he could hear her heart pounding. What would he do now, this man she didn't know? She hadn't yet seen him get angry. How safe was it for her to be in this room with him night after night? Her panic was justified. Finally he turned to extinguish the lamp and then, by the sounds of it, fumbled with his clothing.

She picked up another pillow and clutched it to her chest until she could tell he'd lain down and intended to stay there. Mariah padded to the other side of her bed and got between the sheets. The first thing she noticed was the unfamiliar spicy scent that lingered. She rolled to find a comfortable position and her toes touched a warm place where he'd lain. She jerked her foot back and turned the opposite way.

She would not give Wesley Burrows any more power over her.

Even as she made the silent vow, her resolution was weak. He already had the ability to toss her world into upheaval.

And he'd done it.

Philo Ulrich didn't have much use for him; it had been plain from the start. Wes guessed that Friederick was well aware of Philo's lordly attitude and had deliberately sent Wes to the mash house as a trial by fire.

Keeping fires lit beneath huge vats of wort, mashed grain mixed with hot water, was one of the hottest, most physical chores at the plant. This process, which released the flavor of the hops, created yet another sweet, pungent aroma.

Friederick believed Wes was a man who would leave his wife and child to go seek his fortune; and he believed, too, that Wes had only sought out Mariah when a fortune hadn't been gained.

For the past week Wes hadn't minded laboring alongside fellows ten years younger than him; he was up to the task. Nor did he mind sweating or getting calluses on his hands. This work might be as far from driving sleds through the Yukon as one could get, but he'd never shirked a hard day's work in his life. In fact, he enjoyed the change of venue and learning about the beer-making process.

Wes had tried his hand at mining for gold, but he'd soon decided striking it rich that way was a gamble. There had been money to be made by other means—money that was a sure thing. People paid up to fifty cents or more apiece to have mail carried to remote locations. The challenges of travel and severe weather had suited him just fine. He'd never spent much, so he'd built quite a tidy savings, part of which he'd invested.

What he did mind was Philo's constant harangue. "If a grizzly comes at us, you'll be the first one we call." The contempt in Philo's tone was unmistakable. "But until then, just stick to your job and let me do the thinking."

Wes had merely asked if it wouldn't be a good idea to use a larger wheelbarrow for the wood. He exchanged a glance with his soot-faced companion and went back to work. If Philo thought he could break him, he was mistaken.

Another worker came from the back room, waving papers at Philo. Philo made a dismissive gesture as though he was too busy to deal with whatever it was and pointed to Wes before stomping away.

A minute later the man approached Wes. "Would you mind finding your wife and giving her these?"

Wes wiped his hands on his trousers and accepted the invoices. The open courtyard was refreshingly cool, and a pine-scented breeze swept down from the mountainside. He raised his face to the sun and breathed deeply.

After checking the office and one other building, he headed for the bottling barn. The interior of the building was even noisier than the one he worked in. Steam engines powered conveyors that carried clanking crates of bottles to the machines that filled them.

He located Mariah in an aisle between two conveyors, where she carried on a conversation with a woman wearing a red kerchief over her hair. The employee saw him and smiled, then excused herself and left.

"These are for you, ma'am," he said and handed Mariah the sheaf of papers.

She glanced through them before letting her gaze touch his face and hair. "How's the boil coming along?"

"I'm doing my part."

She slipped the papers into a file she held and tucked it under her arm. "There's something I need to mention."

"Here?"

She glanced at the bottles rattling past on a conveyor. "I guess it's a little loud." She gestured with her free hand. "Let's go outside for a minute."

She turned and led him toward the back of the building. Just as they reached the end of an aisle, a loud ping sounded and an object shot from the conveyor and struck a beam above them. The flying bottle ricocheted off the wood and walloped Mariah in the head, knocking her flat.

To his right, bottles crashed onto the wood floor, rolling, splintering, creating a racket above all the others.

Immediately Wes knelt at her side and tugged a handkerchief from his rear pocket. "Let me press this against your forehead."

She took the cloth from his fingers. "I'll do it. Stop the belt! The switch is under that big fan."

She was coherent enough to issue orders, and her concern was clearly about the bottles being broken, not the condition of her bleeding head. He jumped up and did as she asked, flipping the motor into silence.

He returned to her side. "Let me look at it."

She struggled to a sitting position. "I'm all right."

"I'm going for ice. Stay right there." He shot out of the building toward the icehouse. There was probably another place he could've grabbed a bag, but he'd find a ready supply from the ice machine.

He rushed into the frigid building and glanced around. Quickly he stripped out of his shirt and scooped a handful of chunks, wrapped them in the fabric and returned to Mariah.

She had gotten to her feet, which he could have figured on, but she didn't look too steady.

Shoving the ice into her hands, he scooped her up and carried her toward the door. "Put that on your head."

Mariah's first instinct when Wes picked her up and crushed her against his warm, bare chest was to twist away. He held on, but she straightened her body and kicked.

"What the—Mariah, let me help you."

"Let go of me!"

"Stop being ridiculous."

"Put me down!" With a final jerk, she twisted out of his arms and he was forced to release her. She landed on her rump in the packed dirt in the courtyard.

The anger on her face took him aback, but blood trickled along her eyebrow to her temple and dripped on her shirt. "Why don't we just get you to the office, where you can lie down and we can wash that cut?"

The ruckus had garnered attention, and half a dozen workers crowded around them. Those clustered around spoke to Mariah and each other.

"Are you all right?"

"What happened?"

"Did he have something to do with this?"

Wes forced the ice back into her hand and pushed it up to her head. Why someone with such a stable life and a loving family would behave so skittishly raised a question in his mind.

Mariah didn't want any of them staring at her. She felt foolish enough as it was. All the attention was making things worse. "All of you, back up." She raised her other hand in emphasis. "I'm okay. Just give me some air."

Gerd knelt down beside her. "What happened?"

"I'm not sure how, but a bottle popped out of the line."

"Thank God it hit a beam first." The knot already forming above her eyebrow alarmed Wes. "You could've been killed if that initial force had hit you."

Gerd insisted Mariah hold the shirt-wrapped ice away so he could look at the wound. "You need stitches." He glanced at Wes. "Take her to the doctor."

Mariah grimaced. "I don't want to go into town."

"Want to or not, you're going."

Gerd turned to one of the young fellows. "Roth, run over and let Philo know Wes will be taking Mariah to the doctor." He shot his gaze back to Wes. "You have time to wash up while I get a wagon. There are shirts in the big cupboard on the back of this building."

Wes took off around the corner. He'd used the

washing area before. Pipes had been run from the metal sluices that carried water to the mash house to an outdoor spigot, and bars of grimy soap sat in wooden containers.

By the time he'd washed and found a shirt, Mariah was seated on the bench of a wagon hitched to a harnessed team. He climbed up, flicked the reins over the horses' backs and lit out.

"Haven't seen you here for a long while." Dr. Carter cut the thread he'd used to put four stitches in Mariah's forehead and dabbed the area with alcohol.

Lying on her back with her eyes closed, she winced. "Being a supervisor is supposed to be safer."

The doctor gave Wes a sidelong look. "Bought myself a microscope last year, I did. With the earnings from treatin' Spanglers."

Mariah sat up on the examining table. "Not everyone at the brewery is a Spangler."

"No, some are in-laws." He chuckled.

"Can I go back to work now?"

"You need to take the rest of the afternoon off and rest." He washed his hands in a basin. "Someone should stay with you and keep an eye on you. Head injuries are nothing to fool with."

"I feel fine," she argued, but when she stood and took a step, she swayed.

Wes and the doctor each took one of her arms and steadied her.

She pulled away from Wes's touch first, and then the other man's. "All right. I'll go home."

"Come back in a couple of weeks to have those stitches taken out," he said.

By now Wes knew well enough to stand aside and let her climb up to the wagon seat on her own. She didn't take to coddling, and she sure didn't like his help.

At the big house, he insisted she take his hand as she got down, but then she walked ahead and into the house independently. He walked behind her to the room he'd been sharing with her, and stood back as she entered and closed the door.

"I'll tell your mother you're here," he said through the barrier. He stood with a hand on each side of the doorframe, confused about her stubborn refusal to allow him an inch of leeway. She didn't know him, he reminded himself. She had no reason to trust him yet. She didn't reply, so he backed away and headed downstairs to find Henrietta.

Mariah's mother was seated on a sofa before the west-facing windows, basking in the afternoon sun. At the sound of his footsteps, she turned her head. "Wesley?"

"Yes, ma'am." Naturally she recognized his clumsy gait. "Mariah is upstairs resting." He explained what had happened.

"The doctor said she'd be fine," she repeated.

"Perfectly fine after she gets a little rest."

"You have to go?" she asked.

"She doesn't want me staying with her." It was easy to be frank with Mariah's mother. The tension between the two of them seemed no surprise to Henrietta. She picked up on things below the surface.

"Give her time," she said. "You were gone for many years. She's headstrong and self-reliant. It won't be an easy task for her to ignore her feelings of abandonment and learn to trust you."

"I understand that."

She stood. "Walk me to the stairs."

"I'll walk up with you."

"You're a gentleman, Wesley. But a confusing one."

He left her at the top of the stairs and limped back down and out to the wagon.

Mariah had a whopping headache. Her mother sat with her while she slept, later leaving to prepare food. Hildy brought Mariah a covered tray and set it on the nightstand. "How are you doing?"

Mariah sat up, her palm covering her eye. "I'm good." She lowered her hand.

"Oh my! Mariah!" Hildy darted forward and wrung her hands as she stood in front of her. "I'm dreadfully sorry."

"It's not that bad." Mariah leaned out so her cousin could wedge a couple of pillows behind her.

"You haven't looked at it, have you?"

Mariah shook her head gently.

Hildy brought the silver hand mirror from her dressing table.

"Oh my was right." A good-size bump remained on her forehead above her right eye, stretching her eyebrow out of proportion. The surrounding bruised skin had turned an unbecoming shade of purple.

"Aunt Henny made you soup." Hildy brought the tray of food, so Mariah laid down the mirror.

"Mama believes there's a food cure for everything."

Hildy spread a red-and-white-checkered napkin across Mariah's chest. Mariah picked up the spoon. Her mother made beef and barley soup to cure any ill.

Her cousin perched on the end of the bed.

"When John James comes home, will you tell him I had to get stitches and bring him up to see me? I don't want him to hear about this from someone else and be frightened."

"Of course." After a few minutes of silence, Hildy asked, "Did he do this to you, Mariah?"

# Chapter Eight

Confused, Mariah rested the spoon in the bowl. "Do what?"

"Hit you?"

Mariah frowned, considering the question at length, still not making heads or tails of it. "No one hit me, Hildy. Who did you mean?"

Hildy's expression changed from worry to embarrassment. "I just thought…maybe your husband… maybe Wes…. I know men get angry sometimes. Forget I said anything."

Wes had definitely created problems by coming here, and he infuriated her at every turn, but… She remembered his immediate concern, the way he'd run for ice and protectively tried to help her up. He'd been nothing but kind and concerned. Mariah turned her gaze on her cousin. "Why would you ask that?"

Hildy stood and smoothed the covers over the end

of the bed. "I don't know. None of us know him. I just…I don't know. I wasn't thinking, I guess."

"An empty bottle sprang out of a rack and hit me. Wes ran for ice and showed genuine concern. He took me to town to get stitches and brought me home. Don't let there be any speculation of anything different, Hildy, please."

"Of course not. I'm sorry."

"Did someone suggest that he hit me?"

"No." She twisted her hands together again. "Mariah, I'm sorry. Forget I asked. Please."

"It's all right, Hildy. It's okay." Mariah reached for her cousin's hand. She couldn't bear the worry on Hildy's face. "I'm not mad at you. Come on."

Hildy's hand trembled.

Growing up they'd been as close as sisters. Friends, confidantes. But that had changed after Hildy married Philo. Hildy had transferred her attention to Henrietta. Hildy's mother, Clara, was Henrietta's sister. Mariah figured that Hildy had assumed the tasks of childcare and helping Henrietta because the work made her feel useful, and she felt more comfortable here.

Hildy had lost two babies during difficult pregnancies, and the grief and loss had taken a toll on the once-animated and lively young woman. She came to the big house almost daily, though occasionally she suffered such bad headaches that she stayed home for a few days.

"It's okay," Mariah told her again and looked directly into her eyes.

Hildy managed a weak smile and dashed away a tear from the corner of her eye. "Finish your lunch. Your mama made you custard, too."

Mariah napped briefly before Hildy brought John James to see her. He stared at her with a frown creasing his forehead. "You won't die will you, Mama?"

"I definitely won't die." She took his hand and reassured him. "I'm going to be around to see you grow up and have your own children. Come give me a hug."

He crawled up on the bed to wrap his arms around her neck and hug her gently.

"I'm just fine. The stitches and this ugly bump make my head look worse than it is."

He drew away to look at her. "Does it hurt?"

"I had a headache, but it's better now. Go with Hildy now and work on your arithmetic. You can come back after supper."

He obediently took Hildy's hand and gave Mariah a smile as they left the room. She closed her eyes and tried to rest again, but sleep didn't come.

She wasn't used to inactivity, so the work that needed to be done remained in her thoughts. She wondered how many bottles had been lost, and if the bottling had continued as soon as the mess was cleaned up. A knock sounded on the door and Wes spoke her name. She was actually glad to hear his rich, deep voice.

"Come in!"

He stood hesitantly inside the door without closing it all the way. "Your mama said you're doing fine."

"She sends Hildy up every ten minutes. The poor girl's exhausted."

"She's fine. I just saw her heading home with a basket of dinner for her husband."

"Well, what happened when you got back to the brewery?"

"The glass had been cleaned up. Gerd asked me to stay and give them a hand making sure the conveyors were working right."

"How many bottles were broken?"

"A hundred or so, best guess."

She shook her head. "Anything wrong with the machinery?"

"Doesn't look to be. Once we started up the engine again, everything ran smoothly. Marc thinks a bottle might've settled in the trays at an awkward angle and shot out on the turn."

"Maybe we need someone watching them until we figure out a guard of some sort."

He stepped forward. "They talked about a shield around the chute."

"Good." He'd obviously bathed and dressed in clean clothing. He kept a supply in the bathhouse out back, like the other men. His russet dark hair had been combed into damp waves. "Have you eaten?"

"No. I came to see you first."

It pained her, but she swallowed her pride to say, "Why don't you fix us plates and we'll eat together?"

His eyes widened in surprise. "Yes, ma'am. Be right back."

Ten minutes later, he entered the room with a laden tray. Mariah had dressed in a printed shirtwaist and plain skirt and now sat at the tiny table near the window. It wouldn't hold the tray, so he removed the plates and set them down.

Her mouth watered at the rich aroma of the golden-brown quail and stuffing. Sliced carrots and mashed turnips accompanied the fowl.

"Nobody cooks like your mama," he said with a grin. "I've never eaten like this in my life."

"Hello?" a soft voice called. Faye entered with a pitcher of beer and two mugs. "You poor thing. That's quite a nasty bump you got there. Do you have a headache?"

"It's better, thanks."

"John James is eating with Paul and Emma." She poured them each drinks, then left the room with a rustle of skirts.

Wes waited for Mariah to take a bite before he picked up his fork.

Studying him, Mariah tasted the perfectly roasted fowl. All of her opinions had been shuffled and redealt. So far he hadn't given any of her suspicions substance. Wes had, in fact, been exceedingly kind and generous. He'd backed off every time she rejected him. Today he'd shown genuine concern for her well-being and safety.

He'd been assigned to one of the most difficult jobs at the brewery, and hadn't murmured a complaint. When he spoke to her about his job, his talk was about what he was learning, and his tone relayed a sense of accomplishment. Other men had quit that job after the first week.

None of that excused him coming here under false pretenses, but she couldn't fault him for today. Garnering courage, she set down her fork and used her napkin. "You were helpful when I got hurt today. I'm grateful."

Surprise was evident in his dark eyes. He finished chewing a bite and swallowed. "I know how hard that was for you to say." He shrugged. "I just did what anyone would have done."

Looking into his eyes made her uncomfortable. The connection dredged up confusion and hurt and a dozen other conflicting emotions she had been incapable of dealing with. But she forced herself to look. To feel. She'd hidden from herself and her life situation for so long that it actually felt good to face something head-on.

"You make me feel trapped." There. Honesty.

He set down his fork. Pursed his lips for a moment. And then he nodded. "I admit I didn't think this all the way through. But I've been straight with you from the beginning. I'm not complicated or mysterious. You can probably see right through me if you look."

"What do you mean?"

"I never had a family. I never knew my mother or father. When I read John James's letters, that need to belong to someone came back to me so strong I couldn't see past it."

She said nothing. She wasn't insensitive to the fact that if he'd truly been raised in an orphanage, he'd had a difficult childhood. But the fact didn't excuse him from the liberties he'd taken in coming here. She picked up her fork and he did the same. For several minutes they ate in silence.

She didn't want to sound accusatory, so she kept her voice questioning to ask, "Did you ever stop to think maybe you weren't doing this for John James at all, but for yourself?" Assuming his story was true, she asked, "Maybe you wanted someone so badly that you imagined he needed a father in his life. You needed him more than he needed you."

Calmly Wes took a long drink from his mug. He set it down and wiped his lips. When he looked at her again, his eyes shimmered in the lantern light. "It's plain he has a lot of people who love him and see to his needs. He has a big, loving family." His voice lowered. "A wonderful mother."

Mariah didn't know why his words made her chest ache.

"And maybe I did need him more. But he needed a father. Every boy needs a father."

"Plenty of boys grow up without a father."

"But I had the ability to change that."

Which took them right back to the fact that it was a lie. But they'd been over that before, and arguing again wasn't going to change his mind. She knew that well enough.

They finished eating. While Wes was gone taking their dishes downstairs, John James arrived with his horses and played on top of the coverlet. Felix found a spot he liked on the rug and napped. Mariah unfolded a quilt and made herself comfortable. This time she dozed.

Sometime later, she woke when Wes returned with a book bound in green leather. She couldn't make out the gold lettering.

"What are you reading, Papa?"

"I found a copy of Mark Twain's book, *The Prince and the Pauper,* on the shelves in your study room. Do you know it?"

John James shook his head.

"Marc sent for it when it was published last year." Mariah fluffed a pillow and got situated. "I don't know that anyone besides him has read it."

John James looked up hopefully. "Will you read it to us?"

Wes glanced at Mariah, who nodded in response.

He gestured with a thumb over his shoulder. "Let's take Felix outside first."

When they returned, Wes pulled the rocking chair closer to the bed and seated himself.

"How's your leg?" she asked.

"I'll get some ice later."

"Pull over the chest for your leg."

He did so, propped his foot, and opened the book. The story began with the telling of a poor boy who was born in London. When Wes read that the Canty family didn't want their son, John James frowned. But as the story progressed and a rich family and all of England wanted their new son, his expression changed to one of interest.

As the chapter progressed, Mariah enjoyed hearing Wes's compelling deep voice. John James's expressions were priceless. He eventually lost interest in his horses and propped his chin on his fists to listen.

It was as natural as eating and sleeping to let her imagination slide an unfamiliar direction and picture the three of them as a real family. So far Wes doted on the boy, helping him with his arithmetic at night and telling him stories when prompted. And it was plain that John James thought Wes was the best thing that had happened since the sun was set in the sky.

It was also natural to resent the fact that she had taken care of John James since infancy—nursed him, nurtured him, seen to his care and education, but now the outsider that showed up out of the blue garnered his adoration.

The other thoughts were more pleasant, so she allowed herself to pretend for a moment that Wes truly was John James's father and her husband. Had it been true, they would probably be living in their own house. She would have known him for years, and everything about him would be dear and familiar.

Or would it?

Sometimes she noticed the couples in her family—Wilhelm and Mary Violet, Gerd and Betz; Annika had married Robert only a year ago—and she wondered about their relationships. She speculated about relationships anyway. What did any of them have that she didn't already possess? She had people to support her, share responsibility for her child, to spend time with her. But obviously there was more, or the whole man and wife issue wouldn't have been around since Adam and Eve.

The more part—the *husband* part—was where her thinking got a little shaky, and where the idea lost any appeal it might have held. She didn't want someone telling her what to do. She certainly didn't need someone who expected more of her than she was able to give. There was more that went along with the title of wife, like physical involvement that held no interest or fascination for her. Like emotional intimacy that would rob her of her independence.

She'd observed engaged couples, newlywed couples, even long-married pairs like Marc and Faye. She'd sensed the undercurrent of romantic involvement, seen kisses and touches that made her uncomfortable—and curious.

Anything beyond that wasn't even in her daydream. Nor did she want it to be. She would never put her future in a man's hands.

John James's eyelids drooped and he lowered his head to the mattress. Wes closed the book. "I'll take him to bed."

She nodded. "Will you lift him and bring him close for a moment?"

Wes gently rolled him over, maneuvered him into his arms, then sat on the edge of the bed where she touched John James's head and kissed his cheek.

She threaded his fair hair away from his handsome forehead and pressed a kiss there, as well. She glanced up to find Wes's dark tender gaze on her. An odd tingling sensation started in her stomach and fluttered up to her chest. For a few seconds she had difficulty catching her breath.

Perhaps she did have a more serious head injury; maybe she was going to pass out. She closed her eyes and took a deep breath. When she opened them again, she noticed that disturbing divot in his upper lip, the smooth skin of his jaw and the scent of his shaving soap. The sensation of falling caught her off guard, and she couldn't draw enough air into her lungs.

Wes dipped his head and shoulders forward, as though leaning protectively over John James's sleeping form, but in the next moment his intent became disturbingly...*alarmingly* clear.

*He meant to kiss her.*

## *Chapter Nine*

She couldn't turn away, couldn't close her eyes, couldn't do anything except experience the rush of heat and longing that warred with helpless panic. For a moment, she felt she really might faint.

He leaned closer, so close that she smelled his hair and felt his breath against her chin—and then he covered her lips with his. The contact was a warm, soft touch she hadn't anticipated. A reckless sensation that sent her nerves skittering and her heart pounding. If she wasn't fainting, then this was real. But how could it be?

Mariah had never been kissed this way. She'd never been kissed by any man other than her father and brothers. Wes was no comparison!

Goodness, if this kiss was anything like the ones her sisters and cousins shared with their husbands, she could almost understand their fascination. Perhaps it was because John James separated them or maybe because Wes's hands were occupied with his bundle, but the rush of panic she anticipated never developed.

She parted her lips, only enough to taste him, not enough to make him think she liked this, and eased a little further into the magic of the moment.

Wes hadn't meant to kiss her. Of course he'd thought about it before. It was difficult not to think of kissing her. She had the softest-looking lips and the prettiest mouth he'd ever seen. Every time they were alone, thoughts of kissing her invaded his mind. Along with the sobering thought that she couldn't stand him. He'd been impetuous, but as of yet she hadn't landed a fist on his chin.

Why not? She resented him. She took every opportunity to point out the fact that he didn't belong here.

Why was she kissing him back?

There it was. First the slightest movement of her lips beneath his, a whisper of expelled breath, almost a sigh, if he hadn't known better, and a soft acquiescence…

*Mariah.*

Oh, she was tough, this woman. Tough as nails. Stubborn. Resistant. But at this moment she seemed yielding and responsive. Of course he was taking unfair advantage of the situation. Under ordinary circumstances she would never have been this compliant—this agreeable—this sweet.

With regret and more than a heaping portion of fortitude, Wes ended the kiss.

Mariah's eyelids fluttered open. It took a few minutes

for recognition to register behind her blue eyes. Recognition and shame. What was she ashamed of?

He straightened. "I'll tuck him in."

He carried John James across the hall. Maneuvering the boy's noodlelike arms and legs out of his clothing was a challenge he'd never faced, but after several awkward attempts, he managed the task and got him situated on the bed with the covers tucked around him.

He hadn't given Mariah a chance to react to that kiss. Maybe he'd been a little apprehensive about what she'd say or do. Maybe he'd been more than a little apprehensive about what *he'd* say or do. She took every opportunity to rebuff him. He couldn't blame her, but still it wounded.

He hadn't intended to lean in like that and kiss her, but when he'd been so close…close enough to smell her fragrant hair and glimpse the vulnerability in her delicate features, it had just happened.

He glanced over at Paul, already sleeping soundly, and then extinguished the lamp. Needing a few minutes to compose himself, he took a step back and settled on the nearby chair. Both of the boys' beds were draped with down coverlets. Thick woven rugs covered the floor. Low shelves under the window held an assortment of toys.

In the darkness, Wes's gaze touched on each of their slight forms. His thoughts traveled back over twenty some years to his childhood. To the long, stark room where he'd slept at the foundling home.

Bedtime had been a dismal affair, especially in

winter when the children bundled in their threadbare stockings and union suits and still weren't warm. A shrilling bell had clanged in the hallway, notifying them when it was time to undress and get into bed. It had rung again, the signal that they'd best be lying down.

The principal showed up then, a tall, wiry man who always wore a black suit. He admonished them to go directly to sleep and straightaway he turned off the gas lamp on the wall, plunging the cold room into darkness.

Oftentimes the younger boys or the newly arrived cried themselves to sleep. Sometimes one of them said a quiet prayer, pleading with God for safety or clothing or…family.

Wes let his gaze touch each boy in this cozy, warm room. Knowing these children would never experience hunger or loneliness or unworthiness gave him deep satisfaction. Their huge enveloping family would always see to it that they were loved and provided for. The fact that they didn't even recognize it—that they took this security for granted as the only manner of life they knew made the knowledge all the sweeter.

The only thing missing in John James's life had been a father. Wes didn't regret his decision to be that person for him.

But he wondered what that kind of security and love—what being *wanted*—felt like. John James was the only person who'd ever cared whether or not Wes stayed, the only one who'd looked at him as though he was someone important. Someone loved.

And for the first time Wes recognized the responsibility of having someone who cared for him. Accountability like this was foreign, but he liked it. He had more value in his own eyes because of this boy. He would never let him down.

Wes stood and left, softly closing the door behind him.

Mariah got out of bed and stood for a moment. Her head wasn't light, and she kept her balance fine. What was wrong with her right now had nothing to do with the knock on the head she'd received. Her jangling nerves and thumping heart were a result of Wes and what had just happened.

She didn't want to analyze the experience. She didn't really want to think about kissing Wes, but she couldn't help reliving the unique feelings that had flooded her. Considering the kiss after the fact conjured up a panicky feeling she hadn't experienced at the time. She couldn't stay in her room right now, couldn't deal with this unpleasant boxed-in reaction.

Grabbing her robe, she pulled it on, slid her feet into her slippers and made her way toward the back stairs.

Her grandfather, still dressed in the clothing he'd worn to work that day, met her halfway. "I was just coming up to see how you were doing."

She was glad to see him. "I'm well. I think I'll warm some milk to help me sleep, though. Why don't you join me?"

He turned and took the steps slowly, and she walked

down beside him. His rooms were on the ground floor now so that he didn't have to tread those stairs.

There were still lamps lit in the kitchen and the stove held warmth. She stirred the ashes, added sticks and took a jar of milk from the icebox. Pouring a generous amount into a pan, she set it on the stove to warm.

Louis sat, and she took a chair at an angle to his. "Your face is flushed," he said.

"Probably the heat from the stove."

"Stitches look neat."

She gave him a rueful grin. "Interesting color, huh?"

"Half a dozen people assured me you were fine," he said. "I wanted to see for myself."

She got up and poured two cups of warm milk before returning to her seat.

He gave her a curious glance. "How is it going with Wesley?"

Mariah raised her fingers from her cup in an aggravated gesture. She glanced toward the doorway. The house was silent, so she answered, "I have a stranger fussing over my son, riding along to work in the morning, eating at our table, pawning himself on my family—and sleeping in my room at night. It's awkward, and I resent every minute of it."

He tapped his knuckles against the tabletop as though thinking before he spoke. "I never imagined anything like this would happen. I never thought he'd come here." She met his eyes, and read the helpless regret. "He's a nice enough fellow, isn't he?"

Keeping her voice low, she replied, "The fact remains that it's all a lie. Is he going to stay forever? Is this what the rest of my life is going to be like? I can't help but dread the possibility. What about my life? What about my privacy? I didn't choose that man as a husband. What if I wanted to marry someone else?"

"Do you?" Louis asked.

She rested her head in her hands, elbows planted on the table. "No. I just want the freedom of choice. I no longer have that freedom." She raised her gaze to his. "As much as I hate him being here, at the same time I also live in fear that he'll *leave,* and John James will be left brokenhearted."

He nodded. "As do I."

"What can we do?"

A footstep startled them both. "Plotting what to do with me, are you?" Wes stood inside the doorway, the furry pup in one arm. "Didn't let out the dog before John James fell asleep. I'd best do it."

He passed to the back door, and Mariah exchanged a look with her grandfather.

When Wes came back, he broke a crust of bread from a wrapped loaf on the cutting board and fed it to the dog. He turned to face them. "Come to any conclusions?"

"You have us over the proverbial barrel, and you know it." Mariah straightened and sipped her milk. "What I still can't understand is why."

Wes made his way into the pantry and returned with

a mug of beer. He pulled out a chair to join them at the table and leaned forward. "I've given you my reasoning a dozen times. You can't accept it. Told you I regretted that I hadn't thought this all the way through, and I'm sorry you feel trapped.

"But I'm not sorry about the way John James has taken to me. I don't regret seeing the pride and pleasure on his face. I don't intend to take that away from him. I can't."

Mariah couldn't help asking, "What about me?"

"Have I disrupted your life so much?" he asked. "Maybe you're angry now because you don't hate the situation as much as you want to. Maybe you're even softening toward me."

He was referring to that kiss and they both knew it. Was that part of his plan, too? "You think too highly of your own charm," she replied. "Why should I want to be married to you?"

"You were scared before." He took a long drink and ran his tongue across his upper lip. "But you're more scared now."

"I'm not afraid of you."

"Then you're afraid of yourself, ma'am. But I guarantee you're afraid." He set down the mug. "And it's because of that kiss."

# *Chapter Ten*

$A$t his ungentlemanly revelation, heat climbed Mariah's neck to scald her cheeks. A quick glance at her grandfather showed mild amusement, and that angered her all the more.

Bold as could be, Wes looked her in the eye. "Kissing me scared the wits out of you. I'm guessing that's because you liked it."

Just when she thought he couldn't get any bolder, he pulled something like this. "You don't know what you're talking about, and you don't know me. That was a mistake. This—" she gestured wildly as though groping for a word to describe her hellish predicament "—*arrangement* is not working."

He acquiesced with a curt nod. "I have to admit I'm not all that keen on sleeping on the floor for the rest of my life."

Again Mariah looked at Louis, now listening with

fascination. Her grandfather composed his expression. "Surely there's a solution here."

She didn't have much hope for that, but she had nothing more to lose. She rested her hands flat on the table and leaned toward him. "I'm listening."

"Well." Louis tapped his fingers on the wooden surface. "What if the two of you took your own house? One of the nice ones near town—or build your own right here by the others. You could keep up the appearance, yet have separate rooms."

Wes rubbed his palms together thoughtfully. "I wouldn't mind building a house."

He glanced at Mariah.

She shot her gaze to Louis. What kind of plan was that? Was he trying to force them together now? "I've lived here my entire life. So has John James. I've never had any desire to live on my own. I'm…secure here with my family."

"All right." Wes was silent for a moment. "We could tell your family that it's not working out for us. I could get a place of my own."

Mariah let her imagination run with the idea of Wes living separately, still being a father to John James. It could work—would probably work. Everyone believed he'd left her on her own for years. It would take a saint to forgive a man for that and welcome him back as her husband. "I'll think about it."

John James would be sorely disappointed.

"So there's something to think about." Louis scooted

his chair back. "If you're in pain or tired, you stay home and rest tomorrow."

"I'll see how I feel in the morning," she replied.

"Good night then. To both of you."

Her grandfather stood and left the kitchen.

Mariah picked up the two empty cups. "Why did you do that in front of him?" she whispered.

"I don't have anything to hide."

His implication needled her. "You're saying I do?"

"We both know you do."

Ignoring his comment, she stood and moved away.

"What did you want to talk to me about this morning?" Wes asked. "Before the accident."

She stacked the empty cups by the sink. She wasn't in a mood to talk to him about this now, but this marginally safer subject had to be discussed. "Grandfather wants you to accompany me to Denver. It's not my idea, mind you. A lot of the family is going. Some will come back home while others attend, but I'll be there the entire time."

"Why does he want me to go?"

"He feels I'll be safer if you're with me."

Wes didn't say anything right away, so she looked at him.

His eyes showed puzzlement, but a bigger dose of pleasure. "He trusts me to protect you?"

"Apparently." And if today was any proof, the old man's instincts were right. The frustrating fact was that *she* trusted him with John James's welfare. That's why she wanted him with her in Denver.

The puppy tugged on the corner of a rug that had been tossed over the woodbin, and scattered bits of bark on the floor. Wes got up and shooed him away, then knelt to scoop up the mess. "What about you?"

She wondered if she had more to fear from herself than any harm Wes might do her. "Not all of the men can leave the brewery at once. I want John James with me part of the time. I'll feel safer if you're there to help keep track of him. I'll be busy, but I can't bear not to see him for weeks. Faye will bring him when she and her children come."

Wes tossed the shards of wood into the stove and closed the door. "I'll be happy to watch over him. And help you." He came back to the table. "What all does the Exposition involve, anyway?"

"Nearly every state and territory in the Union is participating," she answered. "Nine or ten years ago a huge building was constructed for a main pavilion, and the grounds cover nearly a mile. This year there will be exhibits by artists and mining companies and railroads, and Wells Fargo is even sponsoring a theater."

"Can't even picture it," he said.

"Many of the states hold their own industrial Expositions," she told him. "But it's exciting to put them all together for an event like this."

"I'm looking forward to it now."

Things couldn't get any worse. Her life had changed tracks so suddenly that she didn't know where she was headed anymore. She was on a speeding train with no stops, no destination, no purpose. Mariah calmed herself with a deep breath. She had a purpose and that was to protect her son. And herself.

She'd vowed that she would figure out what Wes was up to, but for the life of her she couldn't see how he was benefiting from being here, other than what he claimed: having a family, showing John James that a father cared about him.

If he was lying and had an ulterior motive, what was it? If he conned her into falling for him and marrying him, he didn't necessarily gain anything. There was no way he could make any headway moving in on Grandfather's position. Her father and brothers held all the authority.

The final—and maybe worst—possibility was that he was exactly who he claimed and had been drawn to John James with a true desire to be a father.

She didn't want to accept that option because, being honest with herself, it was the one that frightened her the most. If his motivation was exactly as he claimed, it didn't excuse him from being presumptuous or rash, or probably even a little idealistic, but it made him caring and real.

She couldn't handle him if he was genuine. She couldn't hate him. Couldn't resist him. Couldn't fight him. Couldn't breathe.

She might be the only one lying.

Mariah's chest tightened so quickly, she slapped her hand flat against it to force air back into her lungs.

"Are you all right?" Wes stepped in close with out-stretched hands as though to catch her if she fell.

"Please don't touch me," she managed.

"What is it? Your head?"

She nodded. "I'm going to lie down."

Wes set his mug beside the two coffee cups on the sideboard, banked the ashes in the stove and turned out the flames on the gaslights. He followed closely as she climbed the back stairs.

Mariah was deeply anxious about something, and he didn't take her fears lightly. Part of her jumpiness was his presence, understandable, but not all. Not even most.

There was something else eating at her. Something that kept her in reserve and overly cautious. Maybe John James wasn't the only one who needed him. Maybe as much as she hated to think about it and refused to entertain the idea—maybe she needed him, too.

## Chapter Eleven

The next weeks passed quickly. There was much to do in preparation for the Exhibition, and the family worked to finish the tasks. One entire Saturday was spent labeling the remaining bottles. The brewery wasn't operating at full capacity that day, so the children came along and joined in.

A suggestion passed from person to person, and every family agreed to attend church the following morning. When every last one of them showed up, the benches were full to bursting. Toward the end, Reverend Thomas said a prayer for the success and safety of those participating in the Exposition, and the service ended.

Delia Renlow stopped Mariah and Wes as they descended the wooden steps into the bright sunlight. "Mariah! It was quite something seeing your whole family in church this morning." From beneath the brim of a hat festooned with silk daisies, she smiled and turned her gaze to the man beside Mariah. "And this must be your husband. Oh, do introduce us."

Lucas Renlow came up beside his wife, still carrying his hat. Mariah gave him a brief smile. The summer after she'd finished school in Ruby Creek, she and Lucas had attended a few socials and once shared a picnic by the creek. By fall she'd told him she no longer wanted to see him. The next spring he'd married Delia.

"Delia, Lucas, this is my husband, Wesley Burrows. Wes, these are friends I went to school with, Delia and Lucas Renlow."

The men shook hands.

"I must tell you the town was all abuzz with news of your arrival," Delia told him. "Some of us were beginning to doubt there was a Mr. Burrows." She said it with a smile and lighthearted inflection, but Mariah guessed she'd been the one speculating. Delia loved gossip.

"I am very real, Mrs. Renlow," Wes assured her.

"I can certainly see that."

"Welcome to Ruby Creek," Lucas told him, then caught his wife's arm and led her away.

Arlen had come to stand beside Wes. Once the couple was out of earshot, he said, "Delia's always been jealous of Mariah because she and Lucas were sweet on each other once."

Mariah swatted her brother's arm. "You're still a pesky little brother, do you know that?"

Wes studied Mariah's face for her reaction.

She caught his look. "Grammar school," she told

him with a shake of her head to negate any seriousness. "Let's get home to dinner."

Sunday dinner was a noisy affair, much like the night Wes had arrived. Now as he stood behind Roth, he teased the young fellow about leaving some *apfel-strudel* for him.

"My mama made this batch from the best apples in the orchard," Roth told him. "I helped pick 'em, so I get the biggest share."

Wes turned and sought Betz Fuermann's smiling face and raised his empty plate. "I'll pick apples any day you give the word."

"This season's aren't ready yet," Betz replied. "But come fall, you'll be on a ladder in our orchard."

"Do I get a bigger share now? Because my word is good."

Roth turned and plopped a scoop of the strudel on Wes's plate. "There! Now stop cryin'."

Wes grinned and slid a slice of cake onto the plate beside the first dessert. "I've never eaten so well in my life."

Mariah stood near the dining room doorway, observing…watching how Wes had embedded himself into her family, into all of their lives so easily. So effortlessly. They were good people. Trusting. Loving, good-hearted and kind.

*For the most part.*

Annika and Robert stood not far behind Wes, Robert's hands at her waist as they waited in line. Her sister smiled at something her husband said in her ear and turned and looked up at him. The adoration in her eyes sent a velvet shaft of longing into Mariah's heart. Robert touched the tip of his wife's nose in a playful gesture. Right in the midst of this teeming swell of conversation and organized chaos, they were on their own island. Content. At peace.

Mariah envied them so much her eyes watered. She blinked and let her gaze move along. Not far behind them stood Hildy. She didn't join a conversation, didn't smile. Once she gained her turn at the dessert table, she prepared two plates and carried them away.

Mariah moved to the other doorway to watch her offer one of the dishes to Philo where he sat in a gathering of men, including Grandfather, Dutch and Gerd. When he took the plate she handed him, Philo looked at his wife, but she didn't meet his eyes. He pointed to the chair beside him, and she took a seat.

Mariah never entertained the feelings that threatened to ricochet in her gut when she observed them together. Those were walls that needed to stay in place. After a few minutes, she stepped into the room and called to her cousin. "Hildy. Will you help me for a few minutes?"

Hildy glanced at Philo. He met Mariah's gaze almost defiantly, but then nodded and turned back to the men's conversation. Hildy got up and joined Mariah. "What is it?"

"Nothing important. I thought we could slip out for a few minutes and talk about the next couple of weeks."

It was cooler out of doors, where the summer breeze lifted wisps of their hair. Yuri and Felix got up from a nap on the back porch to sniff at their skirt hems. Felix swatted at Yuri, and the bigger dog gently nipped the pup. They took off across the yard, romping in the sunlight. Mariah couldn't contain a laugh at their playful antics.

She turned to Hildy, but the other girl's expression held no amusement. A hank of her dark hair hung over the corner of her eye, and Mariah reached to smooth it back.

Hildy flinched.

Their eyes met.

Mariah held the tress between her first and second fingers, revealing a bruise as discolored as the one she'd had a few weeks ago. It was plain that Hildy had tried to cover it with rice powder. "What happened to you?"

Her cousin took a step back and readjusted her hair to the way it had been. "It was silly actually. A stack of jars toppled in the fruit cellar. One of them hit me squarely."

"Believe me, I know how much that must hurt."

"It's not that bad, really. I wasn't being careful."

Mariah didn't like the feeling that Hildy wasn't being truthful. Hildy's question when she'd seen Mariah's face after the accident had raised a nagging thought. None of the women in the Spangler family adhered to trend by corseting themselves or avoiding food. But Hildy was thinner than even fashion called for. If Mariah allowed her suspicions to form, she'd be forced to question whether or not Philo had done this to her.

But if she didn't ask, she'd never forgive herself. "Are you telling the truth? This was an accident?"

"Yes, of course."

"Your husband didn't have anything to do with it?"

Hildy's already pale complexion blanched. She grabbed Mariah's hand and squeezed it hard. "No. It was my own clumsiness. Don't suggest such a thing again."

"I'm just concerned for you."

"Please don't say that to anyone else."

If anything, Hildy's swift denial had fueled her suspicions, but Mariah wanted to believe her. Mariah *had* to believe her. She couldn't face anything different. "All right, I won't."

"You're heading out early tomorrow?"

"Yes. A dozen or so of us will be there a week ahead of opening day. I'm grateful that you and Mama and Sylvie will be watching over John James until you follow us. I'll miss him terribly."

"Of course you will. But he'll be fine here with us. I love him like he's my own, you know."

"I know you do." Hildy's attachment to John James had never been a secret. After losing two infants of her own, she had lavished John James, Emma and Paul with her affection. Caring for the children had helped her cope. No one begrudged her that bond.

Hildy's gaze lifted to Mariah's. "Your husband is kind to him, isn't he?"

Mariah couldn't disagree. "Yes."

"And to you? Does he treat you well?"

*He would if I'd let him.* Another undeniable fact. "Yes. He's respectful and kind."

"You are fortunate that he returned, Mariah. It's curious, the relationship you have. You seemed content all those years without him, but now, when I look at you…when I watch you… Well, I don't know, but I envy your ability to forgive."

Hildy watched her with Wes the way Mariah looked at the others? And what had she seen between them? Mariah turned away as though to study the mountains in the distance, but she wasn't seeing forested hillsides. Her capacity to absolve had nothing to do with this. Her refusal to be taken in by a stranger was wisdom at work, not forgiveness.

A realization came to her on the warm currents of honeysuckle-scented air. During the weeks that had passed so quickly, her anger had dissolved. When she thought about Wes, when she sat across the table from him, watched him kiss John James's head and tuck him into bed, she was no longer angry.

That crucial part of her armor had been misplaced somewhere between stories of treks through the frozen wilderness and nights of listening to his even breathing across the darkened room.

With that barrier down, her remaining emotions were left painfully sensitive and defenseless.

Wesley Burrows's presence had cut a chink in her armor, and Mariah didn't know if she'd be able to repair it quickly enough to save herself.

\* \* \*

The Spanglers were among the first to arrive in force to work in their building and create their displays. Of course the railroads and mining companies took over the handsome pavilion made of solid masonry and iron that covered four acres. Puffing steam engines pulled in railcars and workers unloaded their riches at all hours of the day and night.

What was by all purposes a little town of western character had sprung up around the main building. The Spanglers had been fortunate to secure a location along the main concourse. Beside them a plump German man had opened a bakery and confectionary. According to information in the guide, he owned a store ten minutes away in the city.

How fortunate that his offerings of ice cream, candies, cakes and other creamy, sugary treats would complement the Spangler's lager and old country dishes. Visitors could eat, drink and have dessert, all in the outdoor courtyard, where they'd be shaded from the July sun by colorful canvas tarps.

On the other side, according to their map, a tribe of Navajo and their agent would be displaying blankets and weaving implements.

Wes studied the map. "We're the only brewery."

Mariah grinned. "Yup."

He squinted up at the vivid sky. "Mid-July and throngs of hot, thirsty visitors."

"Now you know what all the fuss has been about."

She gestured to Mr. Baur, painting the sign for his bakery. "And ice cream right next door."

Wes chuckled. "I'm wishing he was set up now."

"We can always visit his shop in town this evening."

"I like your ideas, ma'am." He winked at her.

A soft flutter, like the beating of butterfly wings, tickled her stomach. "Let's go make sure the ice machines are working before it gets any hotter today."

By the time the sun edged toward the horizon, they were exhausted, their clothing soaked with perspiration. Arlen and Wilhelm, who hadn't started to work until noon, convinced Mariah to go eat and rest. "We've got it," Wilhelm told her. "And then Roth and Uncle Gerd will be here for the overnight shift."

Now that their machinery and products were on the premises, and even though there was a fence and a military guard at the entrance, someone would be present in their building at all times.

Wes picked up Mariah's leather case. "See you tomorrow."

It was a stroll to the livery, but Mariah declined his offer to wait while he fetched a buggy and accompanied him.

As night descended on the mountains and the temperature dropped, the ride to the center of town was peaceful. The sky was awash with striations of oranges and purples and there was very little traffic on the streets.

Wes halted in front of the hotel. By the time he came around to her side, Mariah had already stepped to the ground. "Go on up. I'll take the buggy to the livery."

She thanked him. On her way through the lobby, she stopped at the desk to request hot water. The fourth and fifth floors of the Centennial Hotel had been reserved for their family, but there still hadn't been an extra room available. Family members would have noticed if she and Wes had slept separately anyway. They'd made do this far; they could handle these few weeks.

The bath chamber was blessedly empty. Even though there were three tubs with partitions dividing them, Mariah was glad for the solitude. She undressed and soaked in the steaming water. By the time she'd finished and pulled her wrapper around her, Wes had returned. They passed in the hallway. His appreciative gaze took in her robe and bare feet. "I ordered dinner sent up," he said. "Or we can go to the dining room if you'd rather."

"That's fine. I don't want to get dressed." She heard her words too late. "Dressed up, I meant."

He chuckled. "I knew what you meant."

Hurrying on, she donned clean trousers and a shirt. She took time to brush out her hair and braid it.

Several minutes later, a knock sounded at the door, and she opened it. Wes entered, a towel slung around his neck. His chest and shoulders were bare, and glistening drips fell from his dark hair across his skin.

Mariah backed away, but her attention remained on him. The day he'd brought her ice wrapped in his shirt, she'd noticed he was all wiry, ropy muscle, expected from someone who had lived a harsh life in the wilderness and traveled hundreds of miles with only dogs and his wits.

But five weeks of enjoying Mama and Aunt Ina's cooking three times a day had filled him out. His arms and shoulders were solid, the contours breathtakingly defined. He raised his arm to towel-dry his hair, and she was transfixed.

He turned away to pick up his comb and bent his knees so he could see himself in the mirror on the bureau. His back was as lean and sculpted as the rest of him.

She'd noticed him without his shirt before, of course, on those occasional mornings when John James pounded on the door—he'd been strictly forbidden not to enter without permission, and Wes quickly rolled up his palette and opened the door. But she'd never really *looked.*

Not like this.

He levered his gaze to hers in the mirror.

"You've gained weight," she said.

He combed his hair. "I'd been down with a fever for weeks before I came to the States. I was probably a little scrawny."

"Well, you're not scrawny now."

After laying down the comb, he turned to face her and dried his shoulders. His chest was covered with a dark sprinkling of soft-looking curly hair that arrowed down into his waistband. He tossed the towel toward the hook beside the bureau where it caught. "I hope you like rainbow trout."

"What?"

"I haven't had fish for a while, and mountain trout are my favorite." He looked at her. "That's what I ordered. For dinner."

"Oh. Yes, I like trout just fine. Trout are delicious."

Their luggage had been piled against a wall, so he rearranged the cases to find what he wanted. Securing his satchel, he carried it to the bed, then opened it and arranged his clothing in the bureau drawers.

All the while Mariah watched him, the play of muscle, his fluid grace of movement. "You're not limping much anymore."

"No." He closed a drawer. "Leg's a little stiff in the morning and sometimes it aches during the night, but it's healed real well." He snapped open a folded shirt and slid his arms into it. He buttoned it with nimble fingers. "You all right?"

Mariah blinked. "Fine. Great. I'm hungry."

A knock sounded at the door. Wes grinned and went to open it.

The trout was indeed delicious, as was the wild rice and creamed peas. He'd ordered her a pot of tea, as well, and she enjoyed two cups.

"Did you save room for ice cream?"

She'd forgotten all about it. "Do you still want to go out?"

"If you do. You don't have to change on my account."

They left their dinner tray in the hall and locked their door. Baur's Bakery wasn't difficult to find. Apparently everyone knew about the place, and the confectionary was a popular gathering place for everyone with a sweet tooth or a hankering for a refreshing dessert.

A few interested gazes turned Mariah's way. "Maybe I should have put on a skirt."

"Let 'em look." He led her to a table out of doors. A young woman served them generous scoops in blue-and-white china dishes. Mariah had chosen chocolate with sprinkled almonds while Wes ate vanilla and crushed peppermint.

"Want a taste?" He pushed his bowl toward her.

It looked tempting, so she dipped her spoon and tasted the cold minty flavors. Then she gestured to hers. "Go ahead."

Wes took a generous spoonful of her ice cream and his eyes closed as he let it melt on his tongue. He opened his eyes and looked straight at her as though something earth-shattering had just occurred to him.

"What?" she asked.

"Mr. Baur will be our neighbor for the next two—wait—*three* weeks."

His delight with that childlike realization struck her as wildly funny. She laughed out loud and grabbed her napkin to cover her mouth. Still, more uncharacteristic giggles erupted. She calmed herself to say, "I wonder if he and his family are equally excited about our beer!"

That struck Wes as humorous, and they laughed until noticing people at other tables staring at them.

It had been a good day, and Mariah felt as though

they were on track with the tasks that needed to be accomplished by next week.

"John James will like this place," she said.

Wes agreed. "I miss him already."

She studied him for any sign of teasing, but read none. She'd no more than had the thought when he'd voiced it.

"He's such a clever boy," Wes continued. "He catches new concepts, and his questions show how quickly his mind works. I don't know how to explain it, but he thinks beyond the confines of what is. He thinks more broadly. He thinks in possibilities."

"I know exactly what you mean," she replied, amazed at his perceptiveness. "He asked so many questions about those infernal steam engines in that book you sent. I couldn't answer half of them."

"He'll likely invent something new and amazing one of these days." His tone could have been mistaken for pride.

Arlen had always been good with John James, but Wes took more than an interest. He behaved as though he had something at stake, like a parent would. Like a real father.

They finished eating and he paid. It was full dark, and traffic was still moving along at a clip. Wes extended a hand to Mariah.

His face was illuminated by the light from the plate-glass window on the business beside them. Her heart hammered as though she'd run five miles in skirts and petticoats. Instead she stood on a Denver street wearing trousers like a boy, afraid to place her hand in Wesley's for fear of—*what?*

She wasn't coy or feminine. She'd done nothing to attract his attention or encourage him. She'd gone out of her way, in fact, to discourage him at every angle. And yet she hadn't. And yet he still treated her like a lady, ordering her tea, buying her ice cream, asking silent permission to hold her hand.

Tears stung her eyes and her heart slowed to an unsteadily painful beat.

Wesley Burrows loved her son. He played with him, told him stories, read to him, helped him learn his numbers and listened to his dreams and ideas as though they were the most fascinating philosophies of the day.

He was a good man. A man who wanted a family.

When she reached to place her hand in his, the sounds of horses and a distant saloon faded. His skin was warm, his hand strong and solid. He smiled as though she'd just offered him the deed to a gold mine.

She smiled back. Perhaps she had.

He turned, tucking her hand into the crook of his arm and covering it with his other. They strolled along the brick walkway. She hadn't paid attention to where they were headed and wondered if he had, but it didn't really matter.

He paused, and they came to a halt. "Mariah."

She glanced up, her heart thundering.

Wes glanced over his shoulder, and then walked

backward, tugging her with him into the sheltered alcove of a darkened shop's doorway. He raised his hand to skim her cheek with the backs of his fingers, and her vision blurred. She almost panicked. But then she recognized his unique scent and the moment cleared. She grounded herself in the place and time and raised her hand to the front of his shirt, where his heart beat strong and rhythmically.

She closed her eyes and visualized him carrying her son to his bed. Pictured him carrying a puppy in the crook of his arm and telling stories to her nieces and nephews. She remembered him as he'd been earlier, bare chested and robust with his dark hair dripping on muscled shoulders.

It definitely wasn't panic or fear that throbbed in secret places or radiated warmth throughout her body now.

"Yes," she told him with a hoarse whisper.

# *Chapter Twelve*

Though he hadn't asked for permission, she'd given it all the same.

One strong arm banded across her back, drawing her flat against the long, hard length of him. Her boots grated on the paving stones in that one step. She exhaled an audible gasp.

She waited for a red cloud of alarm to fill her head, but instead a thrill of sensation and expectation tingled along her nerve endings, setting her senses on glorious alert. This wouldn't be a tentative kiss with her son held protectively between them; this would be deliberate and needful. Oddly enough, she felt unexplainably safe in his arms—a security she couldn't fathom or explain.

Her palm grew damp against the front of his shirt, so she pressed it flat and smoothed it across the fabric, feeling his muscles tense.

He simply touched the corner of her mouth with his lips. She almost wept with the rightness of the gentle contact. But it was insufficient, and she tilted her head to aid a deeper, more satisfying union, and he groaned.

In wonder and astonishment, Mariah gave herself over to the moment, to the kiss, to this man who puzzled and confused and aroused her. Tight bands of expectancy made her breathing harsh. Her limbs trembled. Wes must have needed to breathe, as well; he eased away only a fraction, enough for their breath to mingle, and then he used his lips to nip at hers, enticing her to return the featherlight kisses, to sigh, to catch her breath.

His warm tongue traced the seam of her lips, and she opened them in welcome. He tasted like peppermint and a little bit of heaven.

Each new motion of his tongue against hers amplified her amazement and pleasure. She didn't want the moment or the experience to end. It shifted instead, to something more intense when he dragged the hand against her back around her side and rested it under her breast.

She covered his hand with hers, his so much larger, the skin rougher, a provocative dusting of hair under her palm. The kiss waned to a mere touch of lips and shared breath while her heart beat an unsteady rhythm. She focused on his touch.

"We should go," he said against her lips.

Realizing she was standing on her toes to strain upward, she relaxed, loosening the intense embrace, experiencing a biting sense of loss.

Without releasing her, he said, "Don't be sorry, Mariah."

She thought of how many times she'd fought against this very weakening of her defenses, remembered her fierce resentment for his intrusion. And why?

Because of this. Because this had always been a possibility. An *impossibility* rather.

Mariah refused to spoil this moment. Though she was still as uncertain as ever, she had this much. More than she'd ever known. And she wasn't sorry.

He released her to once again tuck her hand in the crook of his arm. This time he smiled down at her, and something in her heart softened. She clung to his arm…and enjoyed the walk back to the hotel.

Since John James would be sharing their room eventually, she had asked for an additional bed. For the time being, Wes didn't have to sleep on the floor. She didn't know what they'd do when John James arrived, but she figured she would simply say she wanted him sleeping with her.

That week as they worked together, ate together and slept across the room from one another, they developed a tolerable, if not comfortable, coexistence.

That kiss had changed things. She was more aware of him, more aware of herself and the experiences she'd missed out on. Each time their eyes met, it was there between them: a silent recognition, a yearning and an expectation. Whenever they were alone, they danced around the memory of that moment and the possibility of another encounter—the possibility of more.

With a wealth of retail stores at hand, Mariah shopped, buying herself costumes for the weeks to come. Gerd had been the one to suggest she dress to impress clients, so as not to draw attention to her peculiarity. "I love you, Mariah, and what you wear makes no difference to me at any other time. But you will be wooing businessmen from across the country, and it won't benefit us for you to look like one of the boys."

She'd resented his remarks at first, but wisdom had overcome stubbornness, and reluctantly she'd acknowledged his insight as correct.

Three-button kid gloves, "jumbo" dresses and horrible masculine-looking hats seemed to be the rage. Appalled at the volume of draping ruffles, cuffed sleeves and the recurrence of the horrible bustle, she nearly wept when faced with the thought of working in their enclosed building and greeting people in the blistering sun dressed in the like.

"Madam should have come earlier in the season, and we could have ordered and altered appropriate summer attire," a particularly haughty saleswoman told her.

Mariah managed a demure thank-you and made a beeline for the door.

"I couldn't help but overhear." A young woman near the front of the store stopped her. She wore a ruffled skirt, pretty plaited blouse and a narrow-brimmed hat. "I might be able to help you."

Mariah was prepared to wear her plain skirts and shirtwaists like those she wore now, outdated as they were, but the girl had her interest. The young woman gestured for her to follow, and they stepped out onto the boardwalk.

"My name is Katie Halverson. My sister Rebecca and I have a shop a few blocks from here. More modest, yes, but we've been preparing ready-made clothing for months in hopes of attracting customers. We've lent our needles to fashion, but not at the expense of comfort or price. You might find something you like. And a little alteration won't take long at all."

"I have nothing to lose at this point." Mariah accompanied her on a pleasant walk to a small storefront in a less affluent district. The sisters turned out to be seamstresses who had thrown their savings together for this shop. They were struggling to get a start.

"Perhaps something like this," Katie suggested and showed her a rack of polished cotton and tulle dresses. By trimming the garments with lace, velvet and cashmere, the costumes still had an elegant finished look, but weren't heavy or outrageously priced.

"You have saved me embarrassment and heatstroke," Mariah told her with relief.

The other girl beamed in delight.

Mariah selected ten day dresses and four evening dresses, as well as undergarments, stockings and two lace necklets. Katie talked her into a parasol and a beaded hair band. "I recommend the milliner's shop on

Martin Avenue," she told her. "The hats are lightweight and not cumbersome."

"If you recommend it, I'm sure I'll find something I like." Mariah paid her and made arrangements to have most of the dresses delivered after they were altered.

"I'll bring my sewing basket to your hotel and make sure they fit," Rebecca told her.

Gratitude for this much-welcome blessing overwhelmed her. Normally she didn't pay heed to fashion, and these ladies didn't care a whit about anything except helping her buy what she needed. "I have two sisters, two sisters-in-law, a mother, aunts and a dozen female cousins." She picked up her paper-wrapped parcels. "And I'm sending them all here during the next couple of weeks."

The sisters looked at each other and their eyes widened with excitement. "We'll be ready!" Katie told her.

On opening day, as was his habit in the morning, Wes dressed early and left to wait for her in the hotel dining room. She arrived a little out of breath, having had more feminine details than usual to fuss with.

Wes glanced up from his cup of coffee and newspaper and his eyes widened. He stood as quickly as the chair and his leg allowed. "Mariah!"

She'd been pleased that this dress had needed no adjustments, because it was her favorite of the day dresses and today was special. Katie had assured her the pale green two-piece dress with gold bead trim accentuated her pale hair and drew attention to her blue eyes. She had conceded to the bustle pad, but it was insubstantial, just enough so that the gold-fringed sash tied around her hips with its bow tied at the back making a becoming silhouette.

It had been a long time since she'd gone out of her way to select a becoming dress and fix her hair. It had been a long time since she'd felt pretty and feminine. She'd had to silence the demons that whispered she was asking for more than she could handle by setting aside her inhibitions this way. There was nothing wicked or suggestive about her clothing. She was dressed like any other woman in the city.

She felt silly carrying the lacy parasol, but she didn't want to wilt under the midday sun.

Wes, too, had dressed for the occasion in a light-weight serge suit, a soft white collar showing above the tailored vest. His hair was still a little too long, and she liked it that way.

"You're beautiful," he said, pulling out her chair.

His comment took her aback, and she murmured an embarrassed thank-you. She had to sit forward to accommodate the padding on her rump. Her grandmother used to tell her she was pretty, and her sisters commented on her fair hair and enviable skin, but a man had never paid her such a gratifying compliment.

"Hopefully I'll survive two weeks of this. Where is the logic in long sleeves and high necks being appropriate for day wear while low necklines and sleeveless dresses are accepted dress for evening?"

"Logic must have nothing to do with fashion. But I have no doubt you'll do better than survive." He grinned. "They had scones and lemon curd on the menu this morning."

She raised a brow to study him.

"But I ordered us both ham and eggs." He poured her a cup of coffee.

"Thank God." She picked up her cup and sipped the strong brew.

"Do you have room for two more?" Roth stood next to their table, and beside him waited Louis.

"When did you get here?" Mariah rose to give her grandfather a warm hug.

Roth held out a chair and Grandfather was seated. "Last night. My grandson wanted to do a little sightseeing."

Roth chuckled. "The beer is substandard no matter where you go."

Grandfather agreed with a nod. "The boy is right."

"I can't believe you took him to saloons," Mariah said to her nephew.

Roth shook his head. "Gentlemen's clubs."

A waiter hurried over for the newcomers' orders. Eventually their breakfasts came and they turned their attention to the food.

Once out of doors, the sun promised a blistering day. The commotion of people and band instruments led them to the main street where a long procession formed. Mariah studied the throng. "How are we ever going to find the others in this crowd?"

"Wilhelm came at sunup to situate the wagons and buggies," Wes replied. "Said he'd be as close to the front of the bank as he could get."

Sure enough, several of their vehicles, two abreast, were already in the lineup. On four wagons, stamped barrels had been arranged, seating for their brood while the procession traveled to the Exposition grounds. Banners on the backs and sides identified them as Spangler Brewery Company.

Wes and Roth helped Grandfather up to the wagon bed and Roth sat close beside him. He had the crucial responsibility of being Louis's companion for the coming week.

They weren't that far behind the Board of Trade officials and distinguished city and state officers who would lead the parade. The Chaffee Light Artillery fired a deafening eighty-nine-gun salute, and the procession began. Having a marvelous time, Grandfather waved his hat as they moved along the street. His silver hair gleamed in the sunlight. Crowds lined both sides of the street as well as the road all the way to the open gates of the grounds.

Wes left Mariah with Gerd and Wilhelm to help stable the horses and store the wagons, returning to find her beside Roth and their grandfather, listening to the opening benediction and the governor's oration.

A state senator ordered the two-hundred-and-fifty-horsepower Corliss engine started and officially declared the event open. Wes took Mariah's hand and they dodged the deafening enthusiasm of the people to make their way to their building.

Those cooking had been there since early that morning: her Aunt Clara, Mary Violet and a handful of cousins and friends. The interior smelled like a Spangler celebration day. Outside the canopies and tables were draped with festive red banners and linens.

"We haven't had many visitors this morning," Wilhelm said.

"Richmond and Danville Railroad and the mining companies are the star attraction in the pavilion," Gerd replied. "Soon enough people will get hungry."

"Stretch their legs out of doors," Wes added.

"And explore the rest of the grounds," Mariah agreed. "And then word of mouth will spread."

They looked at each other, grinned and said as one, "Free beer."

Wes squinted at their neighboring vendor. "Maybe we should have some refreshment before the day gets crazy." He directed a look at Louis. "Care for a dish of ice cream, sir?"

They'd predicted correctly. Shortly before noon, people trickled from the pavilion seeking food and drink.

Among the people who sauntered by that day, Mariah met ranchers, shopkeepers and railroad executives. Late that afternoon, a tall bearded man finished a bottle of beer and introduced himself as an entrepreneur from Philadelphia. "I haven't tasted lager like this since I was a young fella."

Mariah observed as Gerd and her grandfather explained the fermenting techniques that gave their beer its hearty flavor.

The man examined the label. "My partner and I are opening a gaming hall. I'm thinking the clientele we're seeking would appreciate such a fine lager."

After further discussion, Gerd motioned to Mariah. "This is my sister, Mrs. Mariah Burrows." The gentleman gave a slight bow. "It's a pleasure, Mrs. Burrows."

"Mariah is solely responsible for our presence here this year. She made it happen, so I don't want her to miss out on meeting our first new client."

She held the parasol in her left hand to offer him her right. "We're proud of our product, Mr. Simpson. Generations of pride and know-how are in every bottle that leaves our property."

"How intriguing to meet a woman who is both beautiful and smart," he replied.

Wes had a notion to step in and interrupt their conversation, but Louis caught his eye and gave him a reassuring nod. Days like this stretched out in front of them, and Mariah was going to be meeting a lot of men…while dressed in her feminine finery. She was young and beautiful, and this entire event was business. Even if it hadn't been, he didn't really have any hold over her.

She wasn't actually his wife.

The thought put a damper on his day. What was he letting himself in for by caring so much? He led Louis next door for ice cream.

* * *

That evening, Wes relaxed under the shade of their canopy while Mariah and her brothers discussed the logic of laying another track for freight cars at the west end of the brewery. Roth had already taken Louis back to the hotel.

Wes had enjoyed a dinner of smoked fish, boiled potatoes and Aunt Clara's liver cheese. Many of their traditional dishes tasted a lot better if he didn't ask what was in them.

The women served dinner until after eight o'clock, and then the men washed and stacked dishes and sent the ladies over to Baur's for desserts and coffee. Those on the last shift would continue to serve free beer and soft pretzels until the grounds closed at eleven.

Wes had washed mugs until his fingertips wrinkled. "I didn't really know what a huge undertaking this was going to be."

From her seat across from him, Mary Violet said, "You'll be exhausted by the time it's over." She glanced over at Wilhelm. "So will my husband. He's a hard worker."

"There are a lot of hard workers in this family."

She smoothed the tablecloth. "I've never seen Mariah so happy, not since you came, I mean. At first we could all tell it was awkward, and I had my doubts about the two of you. But whatever you're doing, however you've managed to make it up to her, it looks like it's working."

The deceit had begun to wear on him. Lying to this many people was a full-time commitment. A lifetime commitment?

He said nothing.

"Have I offended you?"

He shook his head. "Not at all."

Straightforward. He'd expect nothing less. There wasn't an indirect or pretentious Spangler in the lot. He regretted he was the one holding back.

Before eleven, he had a buggy waiting on the concourse. Mariah joined him, and the others climbed into their separate wagons.

Mariah removed her hat and took the pins from her hair. It fell down her back in a golden wave. "I've been having visions of that big bathtub for the past two hours."

The image her words created in his mind sent his pulse racing. He changed the subject. "It was a successful day."

"Very much so. Mr. Simpson and his partner are going to buy a lot of beer from us over the next five years."

"Congratulations." After a few minutes, he asked what had been on his mind for days. "Have you thought on what we talked about with your grandfather? About moving to our own place, or…or me moving to my own place?"

She glanced aside, as though interested in the buildings they passed. "I haven't had much time to think."

"Which choice are you leaning toward?"

"John James would be heartbroken if you moved out. We both know that."

"But you feel trapped. That's what you said."

She closed her eyes briefly. "I've felt trapped for a long time. I don't know that any kind of a move would change that."

How was he supposed to understand a comment like that? Or a woman like her for that matter? He turned his gaze to the horse, plodding forward, and questions rose in his mind. Somehow, and for unknown reasons, she'd kept the identity of John James's father a secret all this time. She must have been only recently out of school when she'd gotten pregnant. She didn't associate much with the townspeople now, but she had gone to school with them. He recalled their interaction with the Renlow couple on a previous morning after church. Lucas Renlow was a handsome fellow, and apparently he and Mariah once had a fondness for each other.

She had dismissed Arlen's teasing, but perhaps there'd been more to that story. If there had been, why hadn't she married him? Why had Lucas married Delia instead? Wes wondered if he'd ever learn all there was to know.

Or maybe John James's father had been a drifter, passing through the state, temporarily working at the brewery. There had probably been many men hired on over time.

"Where was John James born?"

She shot her gaze to his face. "Why do you ask?"

"The story is that we met in Chicago, right? What were you doing there? Was I supposedly there when he was born?"

"I went there to attend a school for young women, and I met you. We were married and John James was born. You left and I came home."

"Did you really live in Chicago?"

"Yes. For a time."

It was possible she'd met a man there. The thought disturbed him. Anyone taking advantage of a young woman away from home was a cad. "Is it customary for the young women of your family to go away for education?"

"In case you haven't noticed, I'm not like the other women in my family."

"Oh, I've noticed." He reined the horse up before the hotel. This time she wisely waited for him to come around and help her to the ground. Climbing down in all those skirts wasn't as easy as leaping from the buggy in a pair of trousers. "I've noticed plenty. Right along with the fact that you didn't answer me."

"I'll go in while you stable the horse."

He touched his hat brim and stepped away. "Ma'am."

Her gaze lingered on his face a moment longer, and then she gathered her skirts and entered the hotel.

He didn't know why the idea of her with that other man upset him. Maybe it was because he didn't know anything about him. Her secretiveness aggravated him. At one time, someone, some man had gotten through that shield and taken her heart. Broken it perhaps.

He left the livery and walked along the darkened street at a fast clip. Or more likely she hadn't raised all those barricades until after her heart had been broken. It made sense, of course. She'd been young and vulnerable and had fallen for a man who took her affections for granted.

What did it take to earn the trust…to earn the *heart* of a woman like that?

Why did he care?

Wes halted across the street and stared up at the lighted windows in the hotel. Why did his heart hammer in his chest at the thought of her? Why did he feel such anger toward a callous man he'd never met?

Because he'd fallen in love, of course.

# *Chapter Thirteen*

Prickly, stubborn and maddening as she was, he couldn't get enough of her. Mariah set his heart on fire.

At first it had been the boy. And he couldn't disregard the appeal of her big, close-knit family. He'd never been a part of anything that compared to these people. He liked being included. He appreciated being asked to perform tasks and expected to pull his weight at the brewery. It pleased him beyond happy when Mariah's mother recognized the sound of his footsteps and beckoned to him, like a mother summoning a son.

He liked the noisy dinners and the lack of privacy and the constant hubbub. Within the warm circle of the Spangler family he felt as though he belonged.

It felt good.

But that wasn't all. Mariah…she made him want things he hadn't known he craved. She drew him like the moon drew the tides. He didn't know how any man could have loved her—or merely used her—and not have been completely captivated. Nothing crossed his mind that didn't lead to a thought of her. Or a daydream.

This morning when she'd appeared in the dining room wearing that dress, her vulnerability had touched him. She'd been as unsure of herself as a colt on wobbly new legs. Oh, she gave tough and haughty a good try, and if he hadn't stuck around as long as he had, he might have been convinced. But he'd glimpsed her vulnerabilities, and he was convinced Mariah's shell had been thickened as a preventative measure. Inside, she was tender and naive…and the prospects drove him mad.

He rapped on the door to their room, and she opened it, dressed in her wrapper and slippers. She had brushed and braided her hair, but a few pale tendrils around her face were still damp from her bath.

Wes gathered a change of clothing and headed to the bathing chamber. He soaked away the soreness in his leg and foot, rested his head back against the high rim of the tub and closed his eyes. If he were a drinking man, this would have been a night to get lost in a bottle of whiskey.

When he returned, she opened the door and carefully backed away without looking at him.

"Mariah," he said. "When you think about what you want from life, when you picture yourself happy…what do you see?"

"I…I don't know."

"Surely you've dreamed of a perfect life."

If offer card is missing write to: The Reader Service, P.O. Box 1867, Buffalo, NY 14240-1867 or visit us at www.ReaderService.com.

NO POSTAGE
NECESSARY
IF MAILED
IN THE
UNITED STATES

## BUSINESS REPLY MAIL
FIRST-CLASS MAIL    PERMIT NO. 717    BUFFALO, NY

POSTAGE WILL BE PAID BY ADDRESSEE

THE READER SERVICE
PO BOX 1867
BUFFALO NY 14240-9952

# Play the Lucky Hearts Game

and get...

## 2 FREE BOOKS and 2 FREE Mystery GIFTS... YOURS to KEEP!

**yes!** I have scratched off the gold card.
Please send me my **2 FREE BOOKS** and
**2 FREE Mystery GIFTS** (gifts are worth about $10).
I understand that I am under no obligation to purchase
any books as explained on the back of this card.

*Scratch Here!*
Then look below to see what your
cards get you...2 Free Books
& 2 Free Mystery Gifts!

We want to make sure we offer you the best service suited to your needs. Please answer the following question:

About how many NEW paperback fiction books have you purchased in the past 3 months?
❏ 0-2      ❏ 3-6      ❏ 7 or more

349 HDL EZKL          246 HDL EZKW

FIRST NAME

LAST NAME

ADDRESS

APT.          CITY

**Visit us online at**
www.ReaderService.com

STATE / PROV.          ZIP/POSTAL CODE

Twenty-one gets you
**2 FREE BOOKS** and
**2 FREE MYSTERY GIFTS!**

Twenty gets you
**2 FREE BOOKS!**

Nineteen gets you
**1 FREE BOOK!**

**TRY AGAIN!**

▼ DETACH AND MAIL CARD TODAY! ▼

and ™ are trademarks owned and used by the trademark owner and/or its licensee.

(60/60/09/H-H) (60/60/09)

She shrugged. Her evasiveness bothered him. "Maybe."

"What does it involve, your perfect life?"

"John James being happy, I guess. Growing up to be a fine, good man. Me having an important position at the brewery."

He towel-dried his hair and combed it while she watched him in the mirror.

"How do you picture John James being happy?"

"Taking a job he likes. Marrying a girl he loves. Having children."

"That's what you want for him?"

"Yes."

He turned to face her. "Why doesn't *your* dream involve love?"

"It does."

"You just said you see yourself with an important job at the brewery. You said you wanted John James to find love, but you didn't say anything about yourself."

She turned away, rolled a silken length of fabric into what he assumed was a bundle for the laundry, and placed it in a drawstring bag. "Not everyone is meant to experience a grand passion. Some of us have enough to do with our everyday lives."

"So you're unlovable?"

"Of course not," she said quickly. "My family loves me."

"Then you don't have any love to share with another person," he suggested.

She straightened and turned to face him. "I have plenty of love to give." Her tone was indignant. "I love my son. I love my family."

She did. He'd seen her fierce love. He was pushing, but he had to ask, "Just not enough for a man."

"I prefer my independence. What are you getting at anyway? It's late, and we have another long day ahead of us." She turned down the lamp, leaving the glow from one other remaining, and climbed onto the bed.

Wes turned out the last lamp before rolling down the covers on the cot and removing his trousers. He lay down and stacked his hands beneath his head. "What about a real husband, Mariah?"

He didn't think she was going to answer, but finally she said softly, "If you're asking if I can love you, there is a lot you don't know about me."

"You can tell me."

"No. No, I can't."

"What would change if you told me?"

"Everything."

The word hung suspended in the darkness.

Mariah turned on her side facing away from him. She was good at living within the boundaries she'd set for herself and seeing only what she wanted to see. Her strength had grown from taking control over every aspect and living day by day to the letter of the life she'd created.

Vulnerability was a weakness she couldn't afford. Ever since Wes had arrived, her armor had been growing heavier and more burdensome, until it was all she could do to hold it in place.

She recognized her weakness where he was concerned. He pointed out the things that were lost to her—the things she'd never dreamed she'd miss. Or rather, her reactions to him were what made those losses painfully clear.

But she didn't need him. She'd done just fine before he got here. But John James. Now there was where her feelings had first been twisted. She'd been forced to look squarely at the gaping cavity in his young life. Pride had kept her from admitting he needed a father. Pride and fear.

But he did. He adored the man. At first that had angered her, and later his fondness became frightening. But as hard as she had tried to find fault with Wes's behavior, she'd seen nothing but devotion on his part. A future that held them as father and son wasn't difficult to see.

She'd watched them together, so she could easily picture the two of them as John James got older.

A husband? Now that was another thing entirely. A husband was a partner. A lover.

Wes's tenderness appealed to her on a level she didn't want to look into. Her grandfather, her father and all of her brothers were respectful and considerate, but Wes's treatment was more than kind. There was almost a reverence about the way he looked at her…the way he said her name…and how he kissed her.

She'd never made an effort to enhance her femininity or make herself more attractive. In fact drawing attention to her appearance made her uncomfortable.

Wes's attention made her uncomfortable, but in an entirely different way. Her uneasiness was about being drawn to him in return. Every time she thought about that kiss they'd shared in the shadowy doorway the other night, she remembered the sensation of being held against his solid chest, his strong arms wrapped around her. His embrace awakened feelings of security and anticipation at the same time. She'd never expected to feel that way.

He didn't seem to need or demand much. He'd arrived with very little, and gauging by his interests so far, he only placed value on the people he respected and his dogs. His clothing was serviceable and well made, but not fancy. He appreciated ordinary things like good meals and dinner conversation and…peppermint ice cream.

Back to that kiss again.

His questions tonight had been invasive, but she figured his curiosity was normal. He hadn't pressured her. He never asked for more than she wanted to give.

If she stopped deluding herself for twenty seconds, she would admit she liked everything about the man, from his appearance and his work ethic to his stories *and* his kisses.

Each time she'd expected one thing from him, she discovered just the opposite was true. The same went for her feelings about him and her reactions. She should have wanted to run the opposite way, but what she really wanted—in this brief moment of honesty with herself— what she needed was more of him. Enough of him to make her forget everything and everyone else and simply enjoy the moments they had together.

Ordinarily Mariah focused on the here and now, not the past or the future. The future was too uncertain to imagine, and the past was better forgotten. But Wes challenged her to think honestly for a moment. And a moment of honesty was all she could afford. "Are you asleep?" she asked.

"No."

Her heart stammered with nervousness. "Have you ever done something so bad that there's no way to fix it? Something that will hurt the people you love…something that, if you let yourself think about it, would eat at you every waking minute?"

"I never had anybody to love, but I don't guess that's what you're asking." Several minutes passed. "Nothing can be so bad that you can't tell me, Mariah. Whatever it is, I can help you. You can trust me."

Telling him would take more trust than she possessed. Not even her grandfather knew all of it. "No. You couldn't help."

The Spanglers had reserved several tables in the hotel dining room for the following evening. Hildy and Philo were seated across from Wes and Mariah, and John James shared stories about their trip to Denver. "Faye got sick," he told Mariah.

Mariah and Hildy exchanged a sympathetic look. The summer heat and Faye's condition had likely been factors. "I trust she's feeling better," Mariah said.

"She's been resting in their room," Hildy replied.

Wes glanced at Philo. Wes hadn't interacted much with the man, other than working under him in the mash house, so he hoped more social time would change his opinion. Philo attended family functions, but more often than not he and Hildy left early. There was something odd about the two of them, and though he was fairly intuitive about people, he couldn't put his finger on anything specific. While Mariah related with her cousin in a friendly way, she was reserved toward Hildy's husband.

"We visited the pavilion today," Hildy told them. "There are mountains of minerals on display."

"Did you see gold?" John James looked to his mother. "When can we go see the exhibits?"

"We'll go tomorrow," she promised him.

Hildy smiled. "We did see gold. There are fruits and flowers from California, too."

"Can you eat the fruit?" John James asked.

Hildy assured him he would get to taste.

Aunt Clara leaned around Hildy. "I'm taking tomorrow evening off from cooking to attend the Wells Fargo Theater." She looked at her daughter. "Your father is coming, too. Would you like to join us?"

Hildy glanced at Philo. He rubbed his thumb along the handle of his dinner knife in silence. His mother-in-law looked from his face to her daughter's.

Wes turned to Mariah. "Would you like to go?"

"I would, but we'll have to check the schedule to make sure we have a full crew working our building."

"Wouldn't it be grand if we could go at the same time?" Hildy asked.

Philo's gaze slid to Wes, and he responded to his wife. "If that's what you want, we'll go tomorrow night."

They made their plans, and after they had eaten, Mariah hurried upstairs to check on Faye. Her cousin's wife was feeling much better. In fact, she offered for John James to stay and play with Emma and Paul the next night while Mariah attended the theater.

Mariah rejoined Wes and John James, and their after-dinner party moved to the Exhibition grounds. They gathered under the canopies, and the family members on duty brought them tall mugs of beer.

"Here they are!" As the sun set over the bustling grounds, a group of townspeople from Ruby Creek waved and joined them. Among them were the livery-man Turner Price, his wife, Gabby, their four-year-old twins, Marcus and Jack, and their infant daughter. The baby already had curly dark gold hair like her mother.

"She's the spitting image of you." Mariah reached to take her from Gabby. "Hi there, pretty girl."

The baby gurgled and smiled, then pointed to John James. John James allowed her to touch his cheek with a damp finger.

Wes surprised Mariah by reaching for the baby.

Holding her as though she was made of spun glass, his smile revealed his fascination with the tiny person.

"You're John James's papa?" one of the twins asked.

Wes sat, so he was on a level with the boy, and propped the baby on his thigh. "That I am."

His reply caught Mariah off guard. His answers were usually evasive enough so that he didn't lie. He had just told the Price boys he was John James's father. She was careful not to shift her attention. Hearing him reply like that should have been the most normal thing in the world.

But it wasn't. It wasn't usual at all for a man to claim parental responsibility for her boy. Her throat got tight, but she didn't flicker an eyelash.

"Is it true you came from Alaska?"

"I lived in Alaska and thereabouts for a good many years."

"And was you on a whaling ship?" The look-alike brother moved to stand at Wes's knee.

"Yes, sir."

Mariah slid her gaze to catch Hildy's forlorn expression. No doubt it seemed unfair that everyone else produced so many healthy children, while she had yet to bear one that lived. Mariah's heart ached for her sweet, deserving cousin.

Mariah directed her attention to Philo. After glancing at Wes, where he sat talking to the boys, her cousin's husband grimaced. He got up to go converse with one of the other men from town. Mariah eased her way toward Hildy and rested a hand on her shoulder. Hildy reached up and grasped her fingers.

Turner enjoyed a beer, the other men talked among themselves and Wes told the boys a tale of a storm at sea. Before long, the adults had ended their separate conversations and turned to hear Wes's story of the salt-encrusted schooner tossed about on the waves. "The wooden casks of whale oil and blubber broke loose from their moorings, and skidded about, threatening to crush any man who got in the way. That oil was the result of six months' backbreaking work, so every last deckhand worked to tie down those casks before they washed overboard."

The man was full of tales and never failed to capture an audience with his telling. It was a gift he had, this ability to bring a story to life and have his listeners waiting for the outcome.

He'd lived an exciting life before he'd come here. Mariah couldn't help but wonder how the day-to-day tasks at the brewery compared. A flutter of fear moved front and center in her chest at the thought of him becoming bored with the work or her family. Bored with her.

Whenever she'd imagined him leaving, she'd considered John James's disappointment. Tonight she faced the fact that she would be every bit as brokenhearted as her son if Wes hightailed it out of Ruby Creek.

Eventually Gabby wished Mariah goodbye, gathered the baby from Wes and the families moved on.

Wes watched them leave, and then turned his gaze

upon John James…and lastly her. His slow smile suggested contentment. How could that be? How long could it last? He had hundreds of stories. It was possible that five or ten years from now, his experiences in Colorado would be just another tale of adventure he told to a new audience.

Philo called to Hildy that it was time to go. She rose and John James was quick to give her a hug before she joined her husband. "We heard enough from the big hero," Philo said.

Wes studied the man. Several of the others did, as well. Mariah's heart skipped several much-needed beats.

"You all think this fella is something, but he's just a drifter who deserted his wife and kid when he caught gold fever."

"Let's go," Hildy said.

"Everybody's thinkin' it." Philo didn't bother to disguise his contempt for Wes. "I just said what everybody's thinkin'."

Mariah's father, who'd been working that evening, moved forward through the tables. His approach surprised Mariah. A sudden fear for her father's safety consumed her, and she shot to stand beside him.

Friederick extended his arm to keep her behind him, however. "Wesley's a part of this family." He stared Philo in the eye. "If you take issue with that, you take it up with me. You don't hang it out in public and bring shame to the Spangler name."

Mariah's heart hammered and her eyes filled with stinging tears. A torrent of emotions vied for prominence, among them panic, anger and shock. Gratitude won out. She looked up at her father, and warm appreciation flooded her. He had stood up for Wes. He'd given her husband his blessing and seal of commendation.

She glanced to where her grandfather sat, nodding his approval. And then she sought out Wes. He stood with John James at his side, his hand resting protectively on the boy's shoulder.

Gravel crunched as Philo turned on his heel, grabbed Hildy's hand and led her away toward the stables.

A commotion just then caught Mariah's attention as well as that of the other family members. Three boys older than John James ran past along the concourse, chased by men dressed in the dark blue uniforms of the military police. They skirted Philo and Hildy and ran on.

"Why are the police chasing those boys?" John James asked in concern.

"They jumped the fence without paying," Wes explained. "Several of them do it every day."

"You gotta pay to get in here?" John James asked. "We din't pay."

"That's because we have passes," Wes explained patiently.

"Will the police put those boys in jail?"

"No, they'll just take them to the gate and put them out."

Wes had paused in the middle of their family drama to set her son at ease. Mariah covered her eyes with one hand to clear her head.

Her father laid a hand on her arm. "Are you all right?"

"I'm fine." She looked up at him. "Thank you."

Wes sent John James to sit with Mary Violet and his cousin August, before approaching Friederick. "I could have handled that on my own, sir."

"You could have," Friederick replied. "But we'd have been hard-pressed to replace tables and glassware in time for tomorrow's crowd."

Wes acknowledged that prediction with a tilt of his head.

"You honor me and my daughter, and I honor you. That's the way it works in this family."

Wes swallowed as though holding emotions at bay. He kept his lips in a tight line and nodded silently.

As if he'd sensed her distress, Friederick reached to embrace Mariah. She closed her eyes and absorbed his quiet strength before he released her and moved away.

"Shall we go?" Wes asked.

Hesitant to meet his eyes now, she nodded.

He helped carry mugs and trays inside, and then went for the buggy while Mariah and John James waited in front of Mr. Baur's place.

John James had experienced a full day, and he fell

asleep leaning against Mariah's shoulder. Wes paid a young fellow to take the horse and buggy to the livery so he could carry John James inside and up the hotel stairs.

## Chapter Fourteen

Wes paused inside the door while she lit the gaslight on the wall. "Where do you want him?"

"I figured he'd sleep with me," she said softly.

John James roused up, his eyes widening, and looked from Wes to his mother. "I want to sleep on the bed over there!"

"I thought you'd feel more comfortable with Mama beside you," she cajoled. "This is a strange place."

"No, I won't. I'll be more comfortable in my own bed."

Her gaze skittered to Wes's and away.

"I can stand here and hold him all night," he said in a tone belying amusement.

"Since you're awake, young man, let's wash you up and get you changed."

John James cheerfully disrobed behind the screen, washed his hands and face and let Mariah drop a nightshirt over his head. "It's hot, Mama. Do I gotta wear this?"

He climbed onto the cot, and she pulled up the sheet. "If you're too hot, you can take it off."

He stripped off the nightshirt and pulled the sheet up to his waist. "'Night. I can't wait to see everything tomorrow."

"Good night."

"Are you going to tuck me in, Papa?"

Wes stepped beside Mariah, leaned over and kissed his forehead. "Good night, little man."

John James yawned and gave a sleepy grin. "I sure am glad you came home."

Wes stood in silence for a moment. "This is where I want to be. Here with you."

"Mama told me you would be with us if you could. And you sent me lots of letters."

"Your mama is right. I always loved you."

John James nodded solemnly. "And Mama, too. You always loved her, too, din't you?"

Wes didn't let his attention waver from John James's face. "I always loved her, too," he said.

Mariah retreated behind the screen, heat scorching her face and upper body. She unbuttoned her shirtwaist and stripped it off. After wringing out a cloth in the tepid water, she bathed her face, neck, arms, everywhere she could reach to ease her stinging discomfort. Her emotions had been reeling ever since this man had come into her life.

She'd gone from anger and resentment, through embarrassment and fear up to amazement and whatever it was she was feeling now. He'd quickly snared her feelings and turned them into attraction and regret and a hundred other conflicting emotions.

Part of her felt guilty about lying to John James. Wes hadn't known either one of them existed; he hadn't been missing them or loving them. But the other part of her—the part winning out—wanted it all to be true.

John James was so happy. He had something she'd never been able to give him.

She could be happy, too, if she didn't have the truth hanging over her like a storm cloud threatening to burst. She brushed and braided her hair before stepping out from behind the screen in her cotton nightgown.

Wes sat perched on the edge of the bed, and his gaze shot to hers with a question.

She turned out the gaslight, plunging the room into darkness, and then folded down the covers on the opposite side of the bed. It was warm, as John James had pointed out, so she folded the blanket and coverlet to the bottom and pulled the sheet over herself.

Wes stretched out on top, keeping them separated only by the sheet. Already, John James's breathing from the other side of the room was deep and even.

"I can go see if there's another room available," he whispered.

"There isn't," she whispered back. "Do you plan to sleep fully dressed?"

He sat back up and his boots made muted thuds on

the carpeted floor. His clothing rustled as he removed his shirt and trousers.

She rolled away, but couldn't ignore his scent or the inescapable awareness that he was lying inches away from her.

Behind her, his weight shifted, and when he spoke his whisper came from behind her head. "Your father said I was part of the family."

"I heard him."

"I feel like I'm letting him down," he said. "Like I'm letting all of you down."

"Why?"

"You know why, Mariah."

She rolled to her back to find him only inches away. "You chose to do this," she reminded him in a hushed voice. "I argued with you. I told you the lies were crushing me, but you pressed on with this."

"I wouldn't do anything differently," he said. "But I can make some changes now. I can fix things. Make things right."

Fear sliced through her chest. "What are you talking about? You can't tell the truth. It would break too many hearts."

"What if we make it the truth?"

"What do you mean?"

"Marry me, Mariah. Be my wife legally. In all ways. You care for me, I know you do."

She sat straight up. The sliver of moonlight that poured through the gap in the drapes illuminated one side of his chiseled face, along with his well-defined shoulder and upper arm. *Wife?* The word and the idea eddied through her like a warm current. He wanted her for his wife in every sense?

She didn't have a reply. Even if she married him and their marriage was true and legal, there was still one glaring secret between them. He'd already questioned her about John James's parentage. He would want to know the truth.

"Don't answer right now," he said softly, urging her to lie back down with a gentle hand on her shoulder. "I sprung the idea on you sudden-like. Take some time to think it over." In the next second, he leaned over her and unerringly found her lips with his in the darkness.

Mariah instinctively reached for him, encountering his warm, smooth skin. She allowed herself one tantalizing stroke of her palm across his shoulder before she raised her hand to his hair and threaded her fingers against his scalp.

With a soft groan, Wes deepened the kiss, and she met his plundering tongue with an eagerness that caught her by surprise. Her reactions to this man always caught her unaware. He made her crazy, but…she loved how he made her crazy. His scent, his voice, his kisses—he melted her inhibitions.

Somehow, without conscious thought, she wrapped her arm around his shoulder, and he drew her up flush against him. She enjoyed the warmth and firmness of his chest and arms, gloried in the delightfully arousing manner in which he kissed her.

"You're so soft and sweet," he said against her lips. "I could kiss you all night."

"I like the way you kiss me," she admitted. It was easy to confess her pleasure in the darkness.

He eased his weight over her, pressing her against the soft mattress. Her body responded with a rush of heat and a clamoring of her senses, but her head dredged up a feeling of panic and dread. In a fearful betrayal, her heart hammered painfully against her ribs, and she couldn't breathe. She told herself she had nothing to fear from him, but couldn't reason with the alarm that had overcome her. Mariah pushed against his chest. "I didn't ask for this."

Wes immediately eased away and released her. "You're right. You didn't. I'm sorry."

She sat on the edge of the bed, facing away from him, while her breathing returned to normal.

"I'm sorry, Mariah. I didn't mean to frighten you or make you mad."

"I'm not afraid. And I'm not mad. It's okay. Really." She turned and made out his form in the darkness. A year ago or even six months ago, she would never have imagined she'd be considering getting married. A man was not part of her life agenda.

But this man…this one had managed to melt away her resistance and trim the thorns that had always pro-tected her. She wasn't afraid of him. She was afraid of herself—and her reaction to him. She was terrified she might be incapable of truly loving him—that she might never be able to give herself to him.

"John James is right here, we wouldn't have…"

"I know." Her hesitation was becoming less and less about feeling trapped and more and more about feeling robbed. Robbed of the life she could have had. Robbed of everything she wanted and needed. Right now she wanted Wes. "Will you hold me?"

Wes wanted nothing more than to hold her, and he understood she needed comfort, not passion. He would show her he could provide what she needed. If it killed him, he'd prove his trustworthiness to her.

He took her in his arms and drew her back with him against the comfortable mattress and the fresh-smelling sheets. He'd quickly grown accustomed to sharing her life and family. Even here, away from Ruby Creek, her life had ease and order.

Her soft, fragrant hair was cool against his chest, her breath a welcome warmth on his skin. She lay with her hands curled protectively against her chest. He reached for one and stroked until her fingers relaxed against his rib cage.

Wes thought of all the nights he'd spent on board a ship filled with sweaty men, nights sharing a tent in a gold camp, nights alone under the stars with only the heavens and his dogs for company. He wondered how he'd come to this place and this time. Of all the places in the world—or even cities on this continent—and all the people he might've met, he'd received a mailbox full of letters from a little boy who needed a father.

He could've tossed them in the waste bin or the stove…but he hadn't. He'd read them and afterward everything had changed. And he'd traveled from the land he'd known to a place he'd never been to find this woman.

Fortune had smiled upon him.

The three of them enjoyed the exhibits in the pavilion the following day. Wes couldn't resist touching Mariah at every opportunity. A brush of hands here, his palm to the small of her back there. And each time, awareness flushed her cheeks and brought a twinkle to her blue eyes.

There were indeed fruit and flower displays. Wes plucked a lovely bloom he couldn't begin to identify and tucked it in Mariah's hair above her ear. The three of them sampled oranges and figs and dates. Mariah especially loved the toasted almonds, so Wes bought her a bag.

John James enjoyed display cases filled with coins from around the world. Wes purchased a drawstring bag of marbles from a glass blower, and they paused while John James took the pretty glass balls out and examined them. Wes assured the boy he'd show him how to play a game with them when they got home.

The child's face grew serious with concern. "Probably Yuri is missing you, and Felix misses me."

"The dogs might miss us, but they're doing fine."

Wes gave him a reassuring smile and a pat on the shoulder. "Yuri is likely teaching Felix how to catch rabbits right this minute."

By late afternoon, they headed to the hotel to bathe and rest an hour before supper. After they'd eaten, they dropped John James off with Faye and her children, and Mariah went upstairs to change for the evening.

Wes waited for her in the hotel lobby. It would only take him a few minutes to change into a suit once she'd finished dressing. He visited with family members who stopped by and later met a fellow from Illinois and another from Maryland. Mariah would have been pleased at how he spoke of the brewery and invited them to visit their building.

When at last Mariah appeared, the sight of her took his breath away. She'd donned an ivory-colored dress with a neckline that dipped low, showing off her collarbone and an enticing shadow of cleavage. She'd obviously had help with her hair, which hung in a cluster of shiny fair curls from the crown of her head to her shoulders.

"You're the prettiest woman I've ever seen," he told her in all sincerity.

She blushed.

"I'll change and be right back."

The room smelled like her floral perfume. He changed quickly and joined her, where she stood with Hildy and Philo. "Did you get a buggy?" Mariah asked him.

"I paid a driver to take us. Afterward, we can catch a ride with someone else or get a buggy from the stable."

Philo ushered Hildy up into the carriage ahead of Mariah, so Wes stood back. "Go ahead," he said to Philo, and the man got in and sat beside his wife.

Mariah told Hildy how much John James had enjoyed the exhibits that day.

"I was surprised you didn't ask Hildy to take him," Philo said gruffly. "She watches the kid all the rest of the time."

"Only after school, before Mariah gets home from work," Hildy reminded him. "I'm there with Aunt Henny anyway."

Mariah cast a look of disgust toward Philo. This outing had been a mistake. The man made her skin crawl. "If I believed it was a hardship, I wouldn't ask Hildy to look after John James."

"Of course she tells you she doesn't mind. She's not going to argue with the old man's little darling."

Where his jealousy stemmed from, Mariah had no idea, but she refused to defend herself or argue with him.

"Don't spoil our evening," Hildy said in a cajoling tone.

Mariah would never have agreed to attend this event with the other couple if she hadn't believed it was what her cousin desired. The less time around Philo, the better.

The carriage pulled up before a huge building on the concourse. Philo got out first and reached back for Hildy. He practically yanked her from her seat to the pavement.

Mariah cringed inwardly, but turned away to hide her reaction from Wes.

Wes must have seen either the interaction with Philo and Hildy or Mariah's reaction, because he gave her a questioning look. Ignoring the rude man, Mariah took Wes's arm and started forward.

The theater Wells Fargo had sponsored was a lavishly constructed building with ornamental lighting, plush carpets and swags of draperies across doorways, balconies and the stage. Obviously no expense had been spared.

After a man in a uniform and cap took their tickets, they approached the double doors leading into the theater. Young ladies dressed identically in yellow tulle dresses with frilly collars handed out programs and souvenir coins.

Mariah glanced at her coin. The face held a tiny engraving of a coach and running horses. The back commemorated the Exhibition with the year stamped into the metal.

"John James will love this." Mariah tucked hers into her tiny handbag.

Wes handed his to her, as did Hildy.

Philo dropped his into his pocket.

Their seats were in a balcony that hung over the lower level and made it seem as though they were suspended above the rest of the audience. Their location afforded a magnificent view of the play as it unfolded.

Mariah had been to the theater during her stay in Chicago, but none of the others, including Wes, had ever enjoyed a similar experience.

During the intermission, actors and actresses in full costume and makeup visited the patrons in the balconies. "Thank you for coming this evening," a tall fellow who played the part of the governor said to Mariah and Wes.

The next young woman breezed in wearing a bright lavender gown. She stopped in her tracks. "Mariah?"

Mariah studied her, taken aback by the woman's notice. "Yes?"

"Lettie Cox," she said, stepping closer. "You probably don't recognize me as the shopgirl with all this makeup and the wig, but it's me. We knew each other in Chicago."

Mariah recognized her name, and Lettie's features became clear. She'd been one of the other young women in the home where Mariah had stayed when she'd been waiting for John James's birth. Lettie had been expecting a baby, as well. A shiver of unease eddied up Mariah's spine. Lettie knew more about her secret stay than her family—or Wes.

Her worry proved unfounded with Lettie's next words. "You probably never expected to see your old school chum in a getup like this." She laughed. "It looks as though you've done better for yourself than I have. I'm a vagabond without a home or a husband, and you…" She turned to Wes and extended a gloved hand. "You've obviously done quite well for yourself."

"This is my husband, Wesley Burrows," Mariah said quickly. Then she introduced Hildy and Philo. "Lettie and I were friends years ago."

"It's a pleasure, Miss Cox," Wes said politely.

"Maybe we can meet for drinks after the play is over," Lettie suggested.

"We just happen to have a beer garden on the concourse," Wes told her. "Bring your friends and be our guests."

"A beer garden? Aren't you the modern ones? I wouldn't miss it for the world. I will see you later then!"

Philo walked behind Mariah and said in a voice too low for anyone else to overhear, "Your husband is sure free with *our* beer."

He'd always resented her, so his resentment of Wes was a natural extension. Mariah refused to meet Philo's eyes, but over her shoulder she retorted, "That's what we're here for."

The intermission ended, and Mariah watched for Lettie during the second half of *The Cobbler's Daughter.* The play was a farcical take on a romance between a poor man's daughter and a governor's son, with dancing and singing among the townspeople and the factory workers.

"A boxing match would have held more entertainment value," Philo said afterward, as they left their seats and made their way through the crowd.

Wes took Mariah's hand. "Tell your cousin goodnight."

Hildy gave Mariah an apologetic shrug. Mariah gave her a quick hug and said goodbye.

Wes led Mariah out of doors onto the concourse,

where he steered them away from the crowd and in the opposite direction of their building. "That man is one of the most cantankerous people I've ever met. I have to listen to him at work, but not here."

"I know, Wes. I'm sorry. I felt sorry for Hildy. She wanted us to come together. It's hard for her, being married to him."

"Why did she marry him?"

"I don't know." She glanced around. "Where are we going?"

"Does it matter?"

The night air felt good on her heated skin. Overhead the stars were bright against the black sky. She dropped her head back and gazed at the constellation above them. "I guess not."

"Are you hungry?"

She shook her head.

As they strolled hand in hand, the strains of an orchestra grew louder.

Mariah had heard the music other evenings, but she'd never investigated where the sound came from. A stage had been constructed since she'd first toured the grounds, and torches framed a rectangle lined by tables. In the center was a smooth wooden dance floor. Several couples danced in time to the transporting music.

"Would you like to dance?" Wes asked.

"Oh, I don't know," she said evasively. "I haven't danced for a long time."

"Doesn't matter. Just for fun. C'mon."

She let him draw her forward into the circle of light and onto the floor with the other couples.

The musicians played a spirited song she recognized as "They Say I Am Nobody's Darling," and she had only to follow Wes's steps as he led her around the floor in a smooth two-step.

"I didn't know you could dance so well." She beamed up at him.

"There are probably still quite a few things you don't know about me," he replied with a sly wink.

She couldn't help a girlish giggle of pleasure.

"The Flowers Will Bloom in May" was a lively waltz, with a tempo that slowed and picked up between the verses and chorus. By the time the song ended, no one remained sitting or standing on the sides. When it ended, Wes guided her onto the soft grass and away from the crowd. Perspiration cooled on her skin, and she fanned herself with her reticule.

They stood behind a row of tents. Not far away, crickets chirped in the grass along the fence. Mariah had never known a night so engaging or complete or carefree. She owed the new experience to Wes. Before he'd come, she'd only worked and ate and slept, without thinking of taking time for other things that were equally important. John James needed Wes's influence. She needed his influence.

She needed *him.*

The admission was unlocked from somewhere deep inside where she'd fiercely guarded her independence.

She thought of the night before, remembered lying in bed with her head cradled on his chest. She'd felt so safe, so peaceful.

Other thoughts were quick to surface. How long could a security built on lies last? A month? A year or more? A lifetime? But then what guarantee did anyone have when they entered into marriage?

"I suppose we should go see if the guests I invited have arrived," he said.

Apprehension fluttered at the thought of seeing and talking to Lettie again. Mariah stopped walking, but didn't release his hand.

He turned back to her. "Something wrong?"

"Not with you. Or with me. Or with this perfect night. I wish it didn't have to end."

He framed her shoulders with his strong hands.

She tipped her head back and looked up at him. "I wish this was how our life could be."

"Not every day can be about dancing and standing under the moon," he told her.

She closed her eyes with regret.

"But every day can be about love." He drew a line across her collarbone with his fingertip, sending shivers skittering along her skin. "Do you think love could get us through the rest of our days?"

"I—I don't—don't know," she stammered.

"You don't know if you love me?" He voiced the question in a low, soul-disturbing tone.

The crickets stopped chirping and her heart took

over their cadence. A silken flood of emotion chugged through her veins and spilled over. Wes reached up and wiped a warm trickle of tears from her cheek with his thumb. She hadn't realized the moisture had been there until he did that.

He was a good man. Kind. Tender. A man who was easy to love. "I do know," she said.

He eased back a fraction to look into her eyes. His expression in the moonlight asked, *"And?"*

## Chapter Fifteen

How could all this be so easy for him? "Have you done this before? Told a woman you loved her?"

He shook his head.

"Have you loved someone?"

"I thought I loved a lot of women when I was young and foolish," he told her. "Loved them all, in fact."

"Maybe this is like that."

"This is nothing like that." His tone had changed. "You're avoiding answering."

"This isn't easy for me."

He released her, and she immediately felt a sense of loss. "Okay." He took a step back. "Plenty of people get married for reasons other than love, and it works out just fine. I can still make it right and be a father to John James. So long as we're honest and I don't expect more than you're willing to share, I think we can make it work. It's up to you, of course."

He turned toward the concourse.

"Just stop!" Mariah called out.

Halting, he faced her.

"Don't be in such a hurry."

"I'm not in a hurry," he replied. "I'm not going to push you. You have your reasons, whatever they are—"

She leaned toward him. "Let me say it."

He turned over a palm in waiting silence.

"You're maddening and frustrating, and I never know how to act around you. But you're the kindest man I've ever met, and you've been so good to John James that I could cry when I see how he looks at you. If you ever left it would break his heart, and yes, I admit it would break my heart, but I don't see how a life with us can ever compare to what you've done and all you know and have seen.

"When I saw you holding Gabby Turner's baby, my insides turned to jelly, and I wanted to cry because John James never ever knew a father like that. He loves you so much. I don't think it's too late for him. He can still grow up with a father.

"That's not even the reason I would agree to your proposal, though. I couldn't marry a man I didn't care for, and it wouldn't be fair to let you love me one-sided if I thought that was so.

"All of this is out of my experience. Just hearing you say those words…well, that's amazing to me—and frightening, too."

She shook her head as though to clear it. "It's a big responsibility to have someone love you, isn't it?"

Wes remained silent, allowing her to speak what was on her heart and on her mind.

"I think…" Her voice didn't sound like her own. "I think love could get us through all the rest of our days, like you said. But only if we love each other for who we are and not what we want or expect." In these moments, while she was being honest with herself, it became clear. She shouldn't have to forfeit her whole life because of one terrible life-changing night.

"I don't have any problem with who you are, Mariah. I don't care about your past. If you can put it behind you, I'm sure I can. You've already given me more than I ever expected."

"And you won't ask?"

He shook his head and smiled. "I'm a happy man."

She gave a little wave to hold him in place. "Stand right there when I say this part," she said.

He nodded in the moonlight.

"What I feel for you isn't like my love for my family. But it's deep. I ache inside when I think I might not be able to be the woman you deserve." She held up a palm when he started forward, so he stopped. "But I want to be, and that's what hurts me the most. I want to be the woman you love, but I don't know how. I'm caught in this place where I can't bear to hurt my son, and I can't bear to hurt you. Because I love you both so much.

"I love you, Wes. I love you. And I've never said it or felt it before. Ever."

"Mariah." The gruffly spoken word was a plea to release him so he could reach for her.

She flung herself at him. Dropping her reticule to the ground, she wrapped her arms around his neck and met him in a crush of seeking lips and breathless sighs. She wanted to show him how much she needed him, how desperate she was to start a new life together.

He tasted as wonderful and safe as she remembered. When she kissed him, she forgot everything, everyone, and simply lived…loved…felt. She'd cut herself off from feeling for a long time. Loving Wes was like gaining a new life.

Wes eased away mere inches. "So you'll marry me then?"

"I'll marry you," she replied.

"We can do it here in Denver, where no one knows us."

"When?" she asked.

"Tonight? Tomorrow?"

She clung to him, and he swung her in a circle under the stars. There was more she had to figure out—more she had to either tell him—or make sure he would never press her about, but for now she was the happiest she'd been since the first moment she'd held John James in her arms.

"We are really late for our own party now," he said.

She grabbed his hand. "Let's go!"

The smile he gave her lightened her spirits even more. As they ran toward their building, she barely felt her feet touch the ground.

The actors and actresses had removed their stage makeup, but were still larger than life as they mingled with the Spanglers and patrons. Marc and Faye greeted Wes and Mariah with a wave and a smile.

Wes tried to blend them into the crowd as though they'd been there all along. Mariah clung to his hand, and whenever they glanced at each other, she couldn't hold back a broad smile.

Lettie found her and introduced them to her friends in the theater troupe. "Your beer is superb," one of the men said. "I am assuming the lagering process is what gives it a more full-bodied taste."

Wes explained the boil and mash, attracting a few other men and a couple of women.

Philo stood to the side with a mug of beer, observing the different groups of people. Mariah had hoped he would have gone back to the hotel. A quick search, and she spotted Hildy in a small gathering. It was unusual that Philo wasn't holding her at his side.

Lettie drew Mariah aside for a moment of privacy. "It's so good to see you. How are you?"

"I have a son," Mariah answered right off. "His name is John James."

Lettie smiled. "That's wonderful."

"Wesley is his father."

"I'm happy for you." The young woman got tears in

her eyes. "I don't know where my little girl ended up. She got a good family, though, and that's all that matters."

Mariah's heart went out to Lettie and the choice she'd been forced to make. Mariah couldn't imagine her life without her son, and she couldn't comprehend not knowing where he was or what had happened to him. Even with the turmoil that had resulted from bringing him home and telling the lie about a husband, her life could have been a lot worse.

Lettie's surprise appearance had seemed threatening at first, but Mariah appreciated that they shared similar experiences. Their months in Chicago bound them together. Lettie could have passed her by at the theater and Mariah wouldn't have recognized her, but she'd made a point of reconnecting. Mariah trusted her with their confidences.

Lettie didn't want her pain or humiliation pointed out any more than Mariah did. But she was still a reminder of a bittersweet time. Mariah vowed to be more appreciative of John James and her entire family.

Out of the corner of her eye, Mariah noticed that Philo had moved and was paying more than polite attention to a redheaded actress with a bright yellow scarf wrapped around her slender neck. The woman was pretty and curvaceous, with red-painted lips and a low-cut neckline. He said something to her with a leering smile. She frowned and moved away. Hildy remained absorbed by another conversation and didn't notice.

From their positions several feet apart, Mariah exchanged a glance with Wes.

Marc noticed Philo's behavior and moved to stand beside his brother-in-law. Philo gave him a scorching look, then glanced around. When he spotted his wife, he made a beeline to her side and grabbed her by the arm.

A couple walked into Mariah's line of vision. She leaned to see around them, but by then Hildy and Philo were gone.

Wes joined Mariah and leaned down to whisper in her ear. "Tonight?" he asked.

She smiled. "We have to wait for the courthouse to open to get a license."

"What time do they open?"

"I'm sure I don't know," she answered with a laugh. "I should have asked you today."

She turned around and looked up into the face she had come to love. "I'd say your timing was perfect."

Wes couldn't have been more pleased that Mariah had agreed to marry him. It had never been his intention to create a difficult situation for her, but he had to be honest with himself: Coming to this state and insinuating himself into her life—into her family—had been pushy. He'd been thinking of the boy—and yes, selfishly himself—but he hadn't counted on the number of people who would be affected.

He could make this right by being a good husband to Mariah and a father to John James. He couldn't let himself question the ethical questions that might be raised. His motivation had been pure from the beginning.

When finally the theater people left, he got a buggy from the stable. "I haven't rushed you or bullied you into this decision, have I? You have time to think it through, and I promise to stand back and give you room, no matter what you choose."

"Are you having second thoughts about marrying me?" she asked.

"No." He shook his head. "I'm having second thoughts about rushing you."

"I told you I wouldn't marry you if I didn't have feelings for you. And I do. It just took me a while to calm down enough to recognize that. I love you, Wes."

He wrapped one arm around her, holding the reins with the other. In front of the hotel, she said, "You can pay one of these young fellows like last time."

He gave a couple of coins to a lad who took over the horse and buggy. Wes carried his jacket over one arm and they held hands up the stairway, pausing at the landing for Wes to draw her close and kiss her. She had promised to marry him, and she wanted to more than anything. She desired every aspect of a loving relationship. She had the desire, and in her head she knew it was possible. She hoped with all her being that the rest of her was as willing to go along.

"John James has been asleep for hours," she told him. "We probably shouldn't bother Faye and the children by stopping to wake him."

"You can get him first thing in the morning." He knew how much she'd missed him, but something in her voice made him wonder if she was suggesting they let John James sleep for another reason. So they would be alone?

They'd been alone many nights in their hotel room as well as at home, but now…

She turned and he followed her the rest of the way up the stairs. When she cast him a questioning look, he realized they stood in front of the door to their room, and she was waiting for him to produce the key.

He unlocked the door and ushered her inside. She didn't move toward the matches or the gaslight as she normally did. She rested her handbag on the top of the bureau.

He hung his suit coat over the back of a chair and stood in front of her. "It's okay, you know. I'm fine waiting."

The light from the streetlamps and the moon shone through the open drapery, so she was visible as she turned toward him. "I know you are." She stepped closer. "And that's probably why I trust you."

"What do you trust me with?" he asked.

She shook her head. "You're not going to understand this."

He bracketed her shoulders with his hands. "I'll try."

She placed her palm flat against the front of his shirt, and he wrapped her delicate hand in his. "I've seen what some of my family members have with their husbands and wives. The way they touch and share secret smiles."

"Annika and Robert," he said. He'd noticed her sister and her husband, too. He'd picked up on enough to guess that Mariah had had a bad experience, but she wasn't going to tell him about it until—when and if— she was ready. All he could do was show her by his words and deeds that he was worthy of her trust.

"And others," she went on. "It's…well, it's a mystery to me. But I want the same thing."

"You know how I feel about you, Mariah. And about John James. I never had anyone before. When I look at him and see that it's normal for him to belong and feel loved and wanted, I choke up because I'm so happy for him. He might not have had a father around, but he has a wonderful mother and a great family. You've given him more than a lot of kids will ever know."

"It's the husband part that scares me," she admitted.

"What are you afraid of?"

"That I won't be enough for you and you'll leave. That I won't be able to be an adequate wife, and I'll disappoint you."

"I won't leave," he promised her.

"But you lived an exciting life before you came here. All those stories you tell show how adventurous you were."

"All those stories show is what an empty life I had. I was always on the go, always traveling, searching for a place to belong, but never fitting in anywhere. Until I came here. Now the only way I'd ever leave is if you told me to go."

"I won't do that." She gazed up at him, and her blue eyes were soft and questioning. "We'll be following our hearts, right?"

"I believe so."

She tugged on his tie until it was loose, and then slowly pulled it from his collar. "And our hearts will show us how to do other things, too?"

"Only if you want them to."

"I do."

## Chapter Sixteen

Sliding his palm along her soft jaw, he admired her pale hair glistening in the illuminating light that arrowed through the open drapes. He loved everything about this woman, from her fragrant hair and sparkling eyes to her independent streak and her ofttimes sassy attitude. This almost-yielding, but suggestively curious side of Mariah intrigued him all the more.

If she intended to hold on to her secret about the man she'd been with before, Wes was going to have to accept that. There had to be a strong reason that she refused to tell. Maybe, after she trusted him enough, she would understand she didn't have to be ashamed.

She'd never even asked him about his past experiences, but if she did, he would assure her that his past encounters didn't include feeling about someone the way he felt about her.

"I want to take off my shoes," she said, waking him out of his thoughts.

"Sit and I'll do it."

She perched on the edge of the bed and gripped the post.

Wes knelt at her feet. Her shoes were more like slippers, tied on with satin bows. He untied and removed them. "They're so light."

"Not much protection against stones," she answered. "My feet have been sore ever since we've been in Denver. I miss my boots."

He grinned and rubbed the sole of her foot through the silky white stocking. "Stockings, too?" he asked.

She reached for the hem of her dress and pulled it upward so she could unhook the stocking from the clasp of her garter.

Wes took his time rolling the material down the length of her thigh and calf, enjoying the glide of silk against her smooth curves, then tossed it over his shoulder.

She laughed and unfastened the other stocking. He took even longer with this one, pausing to stroke the inside of her knee with his thumb and listen for the quick intake of her breath. She was incredibly soft and feminine.

"You're a beautiful woman, Mariah. These assets aren't hidden under those trousers you wear, in fact those pants show off your features rather nicely. I always enjoy watching you walk away."

"I never did that on purpose," she said quickly, her voice revealing concern.

"That's why it's so…arousing."

She raised a hand to her cheek as though it flamed. He reached for that hand and flattened her palm against his own face. She traced the line of his jaw, and his skin tingled.

He picked up her hem, which was still over her knees. "Who helped you into this dress?"

"Faye."

"I'm glad to help you out of it."

She stood, turned her back to him and held her cascading ringlets aside. He rose and worked on the row of buttons, his knuckles brushing her skin, until the back of her dress parted. She shrugged first one shoulder, then the other, and tugged the garment downward.

Wes held it while she stepped out of the fabric, then he laid the dress over the nearby chair.

Dressed in a lacy white chemise and short pantaloons, Mariah faced away from him. She reached to take pins from her hair, and he couldn't resist kissing the back of her neck and the exposed skin of her shoulders. A delicate shudder passed through her body in response. She smelled so good and clean, like freshly ironed linen and faintly of lilacs.

A soft sound told him she'd dropped her hairpins to the floor. He threaded his fingers into her curls and loosened the tresses until they fell over her shoulder. With one hand, he massaged her scalp, and she let her head fall back against his shoulder, reaching up and back to cup his jaw.

Wes cradled her softly rounded breasts through the fabric of her undergarment and his entire body throbbed for this woman. Cautioning himself to draw on patience, he stroked her arms, tasted the succulent flesh under her ear and along her neck. He intended to take his time and lead them along this journey slowly. No reason to rush…every reason to prolong her pleasure and his own.

Shivers zigzagged up Mariah's arms and shoulders, and her breasts grew tight and heavy. She'd first been surprised at her reaction to Wes's touch there, but then disappointed that the caress had been so brief.

She turned in his embrace to face him and leaned into his solid warmth and strength, wanting to press herself impossibly close. His touches felt good—better than good. His lips on her skin sent fiery pearls of delight pulsing through her veins. He was magic, this man who now awakened her to the bliss of knowing a man's gentle hands and arousing caresses.

Learning this joy was like waking up after a long winter's hibernation. To think she might never have known the wonder of these moments…. "Will you kiss me?"

His mouth came down over hers, searching this time, awakening more senses, setting fire to secret places with the slide of his velvet tongue. He grasped her buttocks and drew her up hard against him. Revealing. Unsatisfying.

Desire was a disquiet that had her waiting…wanting… wondering what it was she'd missed—wanting something she'd been afraid of for so long. *Let it all be just this good.* It would be. It had to be. This was Wes.

He separated them enough to untie the ribbon of her chemise, and she tugged it over her head. He fumbled for the tie at her waist, but she pushed his hands aside and slid her pantalettes and garters over her hips and kicked them away. A ripple of vulnerable panic coursed through her body, and self-consciousness brought everything into acute awareness.

Experience was difficult to ignore, but so far nothing about this moment frightened her. This was so different from anything she'd known or expected that her senses were still catching up with her body, and she regretted her hesitation. As though Wes understood what she needed, he unbuttoned his shirt, tugged the tails from his waistband and dropped it.

She extended her arm to touch his chest. His skin was warm and smooth, and she drew her fingertips down through the soft curls.

He stood motionless under her exploration.

Mariah took a step closer and smoothed both palms along his ribs. He expelled a breath he'd been holding. In the next moment he turned away, used the jack near the bureau to loosen his boots and, one by one, they hit the floor with resounding thuds. He unfastened his trousers next, dropping his remaining clothing to the floor.

Mariah's heart pounded at his approach, but she wasn't afraid of him. She was eager to know more of this wondrous experience. The backs of her thighs touched the quilt. Wes folded her in his arms and they collapsed together on the bed.

The sensation of his warm skin against hers was a delight she hadn't anticipated. Each place where she was soft and smooth fit perfectly against his hair-roughened strength.

She didn't have to ask him to kiss her this time. His kisses were deliberately gentle, almost teasing. She framed his jaw with both hands and initiated a more enthusiastic contact.

Remembering the feel of his hands, she brought one up to cover her breast. Wes's lips left hers and he lowered his head to press enticing kisses to the sensitive skin of the peak, lastly taking her nipple into his mouth.

Her sigh of enjoyment encouraged him to pay equal attention to the other. Mariah saw stars behind her closed eyelids and opened them to assure herself she was awake and this was so very real. "You were right," she managed to say.

He raised his head. "About what?"

"That there were things I didn't know you could do."

"You said you wished this night didn't have to end, remember?"

"I remember."

"I intend to make it last as long as I can," he promised against her sensitive flesh.

"There will be more nights," she assured him.

He found her hand and kissed her fingers. "It's good to hear you say that."

And then he released her hand to stroke her breast, her belly and thighs. She lifted her hips in anticipation of his next touch, a featherlight assault that stole her breath and brought her focus into a sensual spiral.

Every fear and hesitation dissipated in this escalating fever of taut need and rippling pleasure. She was an eager participant. *A willing partner.* She thrust her fingers into his hair and urged him to kiss her again, to keep this keen wonder building.

He eased his body over hers, and she welcomed him. Mariah could have cried for the sheer beauty of understanding the perfection and wonder of a love shared. But she was too joyful to cry, too caught up in discovery to do more than feel. It was a splendid thing, this sweet and sharp desire, this all-consuming urge to weep and laugh and become his.

"I'm going to spend the rest of my life making you happy," he told her.

She framed his face with both hands and looked into his eyes. "I don't know if I can handle being any happier than this."

In the moments that followed, he showed her just how gentle he could be, how ignorant she'd been to think she had anything to fear from him. He first took her hand and opened it against his satiny length, a surprise and a reassurance all the same.

And without a pause in the kiss she was enjoying so thoroughly, he joined them in a slow, sacred movement of purpose and beauty. She accommodated him with an amazing ease; a shiver of exquisite joy coiled inside her. At this moment nothing mattered except the two of them.

Like a balm applied to an abrasion, so were his gentle movements. He spoke to her, though his words were muffled against her hair, and his sentences rambled off into husky groans.

This...*this* was the once-impossible unattainable *knowing* she'd desired. This was how husbands loved their wives and how wives learned passion. *This* was how babies should be created.

In his arms she discovered truth. Mariah learned many lessons about men and women that night, but the most amazing fact was that she possessed the power to make this strong man tremble.

A surprising urgency awakened inside her. She forgot to breathe. Wes understood and his silken intent became deliberate.

Her pleasure spilled over in a succession of labored beats that kept time with gusty sighs and his heart racing against hers.

"You were right," she told him. "About everything."

Mariah woke to the sun spiking through the drapes and warming the sheets and her skin. Heat radiated along her side where Wes lay with his face buried in her hair.

Her first thoughts were memories of the night before. Her body still tingled. She disentangled her hair so she could rise. On her way to find her robe behind the screen, she stepped over their scattered clothes. Pulling on the garment, she quietly gathered clean clothing and put on her slippers. Wes slept soundly, the sheet twisted around his leg and over his hip.

She watched him for a moment, learning the novelty of such an intimacy. She studied the scars on his ankle, another at his knee, and one on his shoulder before admiring the contours of his limbs and his broad back. With a smile, she slipped out into the hall and to the bathing room.

On her return, she found the bed empty, and their clothing haphazardly folded and stacked on a chair. A quick glance around told her he'd left.

Mariah stood before the bureau mirror to brush her hair and arrange it in a loose chignon. She put the finishing touches to a pale yellow dress she hadn't yet worn and added a tiny nosegay of white paper flowers to her hair.

The key turned in the lock and a moment later Wes came in carrying a tray. "Good morning, beautiful."

Upon meeting his eyes, she blushed. "Good morning."

"I was on the schedule, so I made arrangements with Gerd for us to have the morning free. And John James is going with Roth and your grandfather to look into buying horses." He set down the tray and gestured to the teapot and plate of fruit. "Eat something while I shave and clean up."

She took a step toward him, and he captured her

hands and held them between his against his chest and leaned forward to kiss her. "You're not having second thoughts, are you?"

She shook her head. "No. Are you?"

"I'm more sure than ever," he assured her. "I love you. I love everything about you, and I adore making love to you."

A warm wash of satisfaction set her even more at ease about their plans. Until last night, the possibility of such beauty had seemed impossible. Now she recognized the bright glimmer of a future. "I love you, Wes."

He sealed that declaration with a tender kiss, then grazed her chin with his fingertips. With a grin, he released her, gathered clean clothing and his shaving gear and left the room.

Forty-five minutes later, they stepped away from a window resembling that of a bank teller, with a signed marriage license. "To any minister of the gospel," Wes read. "Or any other person legally authorized to solemnize matrimony. You are permitted to solemnize the rites of matrimony between Wesley Taylor Burrows and Mariah J. Fuermann." He looked up at her. "Why did you only give the man your middle initial?"

"It's perfectly legal."

"But I don't know your middle name."

"Would it make a difference?"

"Maybe."

She propped a hand on her hip. "Is that so? Well

then, you might not marry me if you knew my middle name."

"Jane?"

She started up the curved marble stairs. "The judge's chambers are supposed to be up here and to the right. Did that fellow say there's another couple ahead of us?"

"Juanita."

They got to the top, and she led the way, studying the gold script on the wavy glass in each massive door they passed.

"Jack."

She stopped in front of a door labeled with the name Thomas Huff and raised a brow in Wes's direction. "Who would name their daughter Jack?"

"I don't know. Most of the names in your family are German, and I can't think of a girl's name that starts with J."

"This is *it,* Wes. We're about to have our rites of matrimony legally solemnized, and you're making a big deal out of my name."

"How many secrets are you going to keep from me?" he asked.

She looked up into his dark eyes, and teasing him about her middle name was no longer humorous. She didn't want to hide anything from him. "Johanna. My middle name is Johanna."

He grinned and took her hand. "Are you ready to be my wife?"

"I am."

The next document she held was a marriage certificate. She studied the judge's script and their signatures, noting the date. Wilhelm and Mary Violet had their marriage certificate framed and hanging in their parlor, but she and Wes would keep theirs hidden, so no one would see the date. That was all right. Because he was truly her husband, and in her heart it didn't matter when he had become so.

Right there in the wide hallway, Wes pulled her up close and kissed her hard. "Let's go find our son, Mrs. Burrows."

Mariah's eyes stung and she fought back tears. She leaned her forehead against his crisp white shirt until she got her emotions under control. Wes rubbed her back in a comforting caress.

Voices alerted them to people on the stairs, and they pulled apart, but Wes kept her hand securely in his. Two men and a woman carrying a stack of papers reached the corridor. The woman gave them a warm smile. "Are you newlyweds?"

At their affirmative replies, she congratulated them, and the bride and groom dashed down the stairs.

Their building at the Exposition grounds was the central location for keeping track of family members and schedules, so Wes got their buggy and they set out.

Today artists had easels set up along a stretch of the concourse; several of the paintings had been bedecked with ribbons holding prize medals. "If we have time later, I'd love to see the paintings and sculptures," Mariah said.

The sun was high in the sky, a humid wind lifting the flags and edges of the canopies as Wes pulled the buggy around the back of the building under a tall awning. He helped Mariah down, and they strolled hand in hand around to the front.

Several guests sat in the shade, sipping mugs of beer. Aunt Ina stood in the doorway, her sharp gaze landing on Wes and Mariah. She mopped her forehead with the hem of her apron. "Do you know what happened?"

"What's happened?" Mariah asked, and her first panicked thought was that John James or her grandfather had been in an accident. "Is John James all right?"

"As far as I know he's fine," she replied. "But Clara found Hildy on the floor in her room this morning."

Hildy! "Is she all right?"

"I don't know. They called a doctor and he had her taken to the Sisters of Charity Ward, where she could be looked after. Clara's with her. I saw Hildy when they carried her out, Mariah." She got tears in her eyes. "She looked bad."

Mariah guided her inside where it was marginally cooler. "You should probably rest. Wes can take over your shift, can't you, Wes?" She glanced up at him.

"Yes, ma'am. I'd be glad to."

"I need to go be with Clara." Ina mopped her eyes with her apron hem. "It's that man, Mariah. Her mother's always had a bad feeling about him, but Hildy won't hear it when Clara asks questions."

Mariah had more than a bad feeling about Philo, and she dreaded hearing what had happened to her cousin.

"You take your aunt to the hotel to freshen up, and then see if you can visit Hildy," Wes told her. "Take the buggy."

Mariah gave him a grateful nod. He hugged her, and she helped Ina gather her things and they headed for the hotel.

"If it's all the same, I think I'll nap an hour," Ina told her on their way into the hotel.

"Of course." Once she'd seen Ina to her room, she asked directions to the Sisters of Charity, which she followed until she reached a narrow brick street.

The hospital was a gray stone building with two levels. The smell of ammonia didn't disguise the sour stench that stung Mariah's nose. She was directed along a hallway, where she kept her gaze fixed straight ahead without looking into the rooms she passed. She heard moaning from the interior of one and cursing from another.

The nun showed her into a dimly lit room and turned away, her shoes squeaking along the tiled corridor.

Aunt Clara sat on a wooden chair beside a cot, holding the hand of someone Mariah didn't recognize.

Hildy's features were swollen and bruised. She had a cut above one eye and her arm was bandaged in plaster. Horror rose up in Mariah's throat, and she had to swallow hard to fight it down.

"Aunt Clara?"

Her aunt looked up. Her lower lip trembled. "He did this to her."

# Chapter Seventeen

"Philo is nowhere to be found," Clara said, "but he did this to her. You saw him last night."

Oh, she'd seen him last night, and she'd been nothing but eager to get away.

Clara dabbed her nose with a hanky. "One of the hotel residents on the third floor complained at the desk last night that there was a racket going on up above. The man at the desk checked it out and said Philo answered the door and told him a table had broken. He said he'd pay for it in the morning. The rest of us were still at the Exhibition when this happened to her."

Mariah and Wes had come back to the hotel before the others, but Hildy's room was halfway down the hall from theirs.

"Patrick and Marc are looking for him. They told the marshal what we believe happened, but he wasn't helpful."

"Has she spoken?" Mariah asked.

Clara shook her head and sobbed. "She hasn't been awake."

"At all?"

"Not at all." She raised the sodden handkerchief to her face and swabbed tears. "The doctors said she might have something wrong with her brain."

All the air sucked from Mariah's lungs. The room blurred, and she reached blindly, grasping the foot of the metal bed and keeping herself upright.

"Sit down, honey." Clara got up and gave Mariah her chair. She found another and pulled it across the floor.

As soon as her vision cleared, Mariah leaned forward to take Hildy's delicate pale hand and press it to her cheek. A thousand regrets welled up and consumed her. Even through her tears, it hurt to look at her cousin's puffy, battered face. "Is that arm broken?"

Clara nodded. "They packed it in ice and only set it about an hour ago. I guess it's a blessing she's not awake and in pain, but I'm scared."

Mariah laid her face on Hildy's shoulder and cried. "I'm sorry. I'm so sorry."

Regret became a living, breathing thing inside her. She'd seen Philo's behavior the night before. Because she'd been eager to get away, she'd ignored the signs. "I should have known."

"We all suspected something was wrong."

"But I should have *known*," Mariah cried in anguish.

"You couldn't have," Clara assured her.

Though seeing her was torture, she kept her eyes

on her cousin's face. She would not leave Hildy's side. She'd sit right here and will energy into her until Hildy woke up.

It was, after all, her fault this had happened.

Roth brought John James to Wes that afternoon, and Wes kept him busy in the kitchen. Later, he took him next door for ice cream. Wes assigned the child manageable chores while they finished supper dishes. Roth's mother was planning to take Emma and Paul for the evening, and she asked if John James could accompany them.

Wes agreed he'd have a better time with the other children than waiting around for him. He took him for a stroll along the concourse first.

"Where's Mama?"

"She's with Hildy at the hospital."

"Is Hildy going to get better?"

Wes had heard the bad reports from other family members. "The doctors are taking good care of her. She's at the best place she can be right now."

"Maybe I can go see her."

"Maybe in a few days. I'll come get you when I'm done here tonight, all right?"

"All right."

Annika and Robert arrived to take a shift, so Wes left and visited the hospital. He got as far as the hallway outside Hildy's room.

Marc and Patrick, Hildy's brother and father, blocked his way. "We haven't found Philo yet," Patrick said.

"We've checked around, think he might be in the clubs or saloons. We're going to eat and then go looking."

"I'll come with you," Wes told him. "I thought I'd talk to Mariah first. Maybe take her to dinner."

Marc inclined his head. "You can try."

Wes entered the room where Clara and Mary Violet held their vigil seated on wooden chairs. His new wife was on her knees beside the narrow cot, holding Hildy's hand. He wasn't sure which sight distressed him more: Hildy's grotesquely discolored face or Mariah's red and puffy eyes and nose.

Wes stepped closer and said softly, "Mariah?"

Mary Violet and Clara slid their chairs aside, so he could get close.

Sensitive to her distress, he hunkered down beside her. "Mariah?"

"This is my fault." Her voice was hoarse from crying. She turned her mournful blue gaze on him, and his chest tightened. It was her wedding day, and here she was making herself sick by taking responsibility for something that couldn't possibly be her fault.

"I know how much you love her," he said. "Everyone loves Hildy. But this isn't your fault. She didn't ask anyone for help or let anyone know how bad things were."

"I should have known."

He exchanged a look with Clara before asking, "Had she told you Philo hit her?"

Mariah shook her head and glanced at her aunt. "She hid it. We figured out that all along she's been hiding the bruises and telling us she was staying home with terrible headaches. I let her get by with those lies."

"Darling, why don't you come have something to eat with me?" He rested his hand on her arm. "We'll get a meal nearby."

She pulled away from his touch. "I'm not hungry. I'm staying here."

He looked at Mary Violet, and she shrugged. "She hasn't moved from that spot all day."

If Mariah was determined to stay with her cousin, Wes couldn't pick her up and carry her out screaming. She knew what she wanted. "I'll bring you something."

She didn't reply.

He looked around, scoured the hall and located another chair, which he brought to Hildy's bedside. "Sit here," he insisted.

He took the hand she raised and helped her up. She scooted the chair as close as possible and sat, once again taking Hildy's hand.

"Have you eaten?" he asked Clara and Ina.

"Patrick brought us sandwiches," Ina told him. "Mariah wouldn't touch hers."

Patrick and Marc waited in the hallway. A muscle ticked in Patrick's jaw. "I know how she feels. I'm kicking myself right about now, too. A man ought not let something like this happen to his daughter."

They ate in glum silence in a café across the street from the hospital, and Wes paid for soup, a slice of buttered bread and milk to carry back to Mariah.

She nibbled at the bread, but used the spoon to cautiously trickle tiny portions of the soup between Hildy's lips.

They didn't find Philo that night. Wes took Clara and Patrick's day shifts for the two days that followed, and at night he joined the men in scouring the city.

Faye and Mary Violet prepared to take the children home to Ruby Creek. At the train station, Wes knelt down to John James. "Take good care of Yuri for me when you get home. Mama and I will be there shortly."

"And Hildy, too."

"That's what we're all praying for, buddy."

John James wrapped his arms around Wes's neck. The little boy smelled like clean laundry and out-of-doors, and his hair was soft against Wes's cheek. "I love you, Papa."

"And I love you," he answered, his words thick with emotion. "You be a good boy for your aunts now."

Wes watched them board the passenger car and minutes later waved back at John James who grinned from the window.

Mariah's distress for her cousin, at the expense of everything else, including seeing John James off, was disturbing. Wes was at a loss to know how to fix it, except to be there for her.

After three days and nights, Mariah collapsed in exhaustion. Wes caught her before she struck the floor. He carried her to the buggy, then through the hotel lobby and up to their room, where he placed her on the bed.

She still wore the pale yellow dress she'd worn when they'd said their marriage vows. He removed her shoes and stockings, unbuttoned her wrinkled dress and tugged away as many clothes as he could manage before bathing her face and hands with fresh water.

Tucking the sheet around her, he closed the drapes and sat nearby to wait. He went out occasionally, making certain the shifts were covered at the beer garden. That evening Louis came to the room, and Wes ushered him in.

"How is she?" Louis asked.

"Still sleeping," he answered softly. He lit the lamp on the wall, keeping the flame low, and ushered her grandfather to the side of the bed.

Louis studied her sleeping form. Her skin was paler than usual, and her lashes rested against the dark hollows under her eyes. "I love all of my children and grandchildren," Louis said. "Great-grandchildren, too. And as much as we try not to have favorites, some just latch on to your heart in a real special way."

Wes got him a chair. Louis backed onto the cushioned seat awkwardly.

Wes sat facing him. "Yes, sir."

"This is a real mess, this business with Hildy and Philo. Mariah's taking it real hard." Tears welled in Louis's eyes. "Real hard."

"For some reason she's blaming herself," Wes replied.

"I guess we all pretty much feel to blame for not figuring it out sooner."

Wes could only nod.

"I'm real glad you came home, son," Louis said, lifting his gaze to Wes's. "She missed you, and John James needed his father. It's a good thing you did, coming home. It's plain to see how she feels about you. Your heart is on your sleeve, young fellow."

Over the last several weeks Louis's grasp on reality had teetered back and forth on the subject of Wes's presence. Most times the old man spoke as though Wes had truly been Mariah's husband all along. Wes figured it was better he take that road than to accidentally tell someone the other story.

"I love her," Wes told him. "I'm going to do everything in my power to make the two of them happy." He considered the wisdom of telling Louis that they'd been married the morning before they'd learned about Hildy. He glanced at Mariah. She should have a say, however, so he kept silent. If Louis believed they'd been married all along, the news might confuse him.

A few minutes later, Wes walked Louis down the hall to his room, and then returned. Eventually he undressed and got into bed. He took Mariah in his arms and she snuggled close without waking.

He woke at dawn and eased out of bed without disturbing Mariah so he could wash and shave. He left for five minutes to order breakfast and have coffee sent up. When he returned, her eyes opened.

She stared at him, focusing, then blinked and looked toward the window.

"Good morning," he said.

Her gaze fixed on him. She seemed rested, but it only took moments for that look of tortured regret to return to her eyes. "I didn't dream it."

"You didn't dream it. I'll go and get a tub ready for you in the bath chamber. You'll feel better after you've bathed and washed your hair. I'll help you."

She rocked her head back and forth on the pillow. "I won't feel better."

"Well, you'll feel clean. And I've ordered coffee and some breakfast."

"I'm not—"

"Don't say it. You're going to bathe and eat and put on clean clothing. You're not doing Hildy any good by starving yourself."

He heated water and returned for her, helping her out of her undergarments and into the steaming tub. He poured pitchers full over her hair until it was soaked, then lathered and massaged the wet locks and her scalp.

"I'm not like this," she said, reaching to wipe dripping suds from her jaw. "I'm stronger than this."

"You're the strongest woman I know," he answered, still enjoying the feel of her thick, soapy hair between his fingers. "I've never washed a woman's hair before."

She said nothing.

"I kind of like it."

Once he had her hair rinsed free of suds, he gave her a towel to wrap it and had her stand so he could wash her.

With every tender caress of the soapy cloth, another fissure widened in Mariah's breaking heart. There was nothing sexual about the way he cared for her. He respectfully took care of her needs as though she was a needy child.

He wouldn't be able to look at her body or attend to her like this if he knew. He would never have made her his wife, would never have made love to her in the tender way he had. Wes never would have loved her....

The air had cooled her wet face, so the tears that trailed her cheek scalded.

"Let's dry you off, darling." He dried her tears. Her body. Wrapped her in toweling and then her wrapper. "It breaks my heart to see you this way."

"You wouldn't be doing this if you knew," she said. "You wouldn't love me. You would never forgive me."

Her statement confused him, but she was distressed and not herself. He picked her up and swiftly carried her down the hallway and into their room. "Our breakfast is here."

"I can't eat."

"You're going to eat." His tone held a firmness that told her his tolerance had limits. He set her down on a chair near the small table.

"Will you check and see if there's been any change?"

He understood she was asking about Hildy. "I will if you eat while I'm gone."

She nodded, and the towel tumbled loose.

He took it from her head and dabbed at the ends of

her hair, then brought her comb from the bureau. "Can you do this?"

She nodded.

"And eat." He grabbed his hat. "I'll be back soon."

Her arms had never been so heavy, her fingers so clumsy, but she raised the comb and started at the ends of her hair, untangling and smoothing. It was a mindless task, one she'd performed hundreds of times. She finished and looked at the tray he'd set nearby.

She pulled it closer and removed the cover. The smell of bacon and eggs made her belly rumble. How long had it been since she'd eaten? Picking up a fork, she took a few bites and tasted nothing. Her hand shook as she poured coffee, and the liquid slopped over onto the tray. She added sugar to her cup and drank half.

Her stomach felt full. Setting down the cup, she closed her eyes. Normal everyday things. Eating. Drinking. Bathing. What did any of it matter, really? What difference did anything make if you couldn't protect the people you loved?

She had done Hildy an unforgivable injustice. What if she never had the opportunity to make it up to her? To apologize? What if Hildy never woke up?

Her mind attacked her conscience with memories of Hildy as a young girl, with visions of how her lively nature had been oppressed over time. She'd never recovered after grieving the loss of those babies. For days she'd locked herself away in their little house, declining help, refusing comfort.

More images superimposed themselves over those of Hildy. Images of Philo's angry face, his sneer, that threatening stance and the feel of his painful grip.

*He'd been the reason Hildy's babies had died.* It became glaringly clear now that Hildy had shut herself away every time she'd been bruised and battered—and she'd been so after giving birth to babies too tiny to live.

Anger welled up in Mariah. Anger and regret and guilt so severe, so devastating she couldn't bear the weight that consumed her. With a cry, she lunged and swept the tray from the table. Plates and food and glassware clattered and spilled in a deafening crash, but she didn't hear it. She heard nothing but the keening wail of disappointment and fury that rose from her very being and tore from her throat.

She dropped from her seat to her knees on the rug, where she pounded her fists and shouted, "No! No! No! No!"

Vaguely aware of the door being thrown open, she ignored Wes when he spoke and knelt down beside her. She buried her face in her hands and wept from her soul. Deep, gut-wrenching sobs that burst out of her like water from a broken dam.

Wes wrapped a rag around her hand, but the fact barely registered that she'd cut herself on one of the shards of china. No pain was as great as the one she suffered by being responsible for her cousin losing her babies. Nothing hurt as much as seeing Hildy lying at the very precipice of death and knowing she could have done something. "I could have prevented all of it," she wailed.

"Mariah," Wes said, urging her to stand.

She wouldn't have any part of his comfort this time. "It's my fault she's in that hospital." She was fierce in her pronouncement. She grabbed his forearms and looked him straight in the eye. They were both on their knees in the chaos of the spattered breakfast. "I could have told the truth and stopped her from marrying him. But I didn't."

"And what *is* the truth, Mariah? How could anything you might have said kept Hildy from marrying him?"

She deserved this punishing shame. She'd never been so furious. At any moment her skin would burst from the pressure of holding in pain and anger and remorse. If she didn't let it go now, she would shatter into a million pieces.

Her fingers trembled on his strong forearms, but she didn't loosen her grip. And she didn't look away. "It was Philo," she said. "We—he—it happened the night before their wedding. He is John James's father."

# Chapter Eighteen

Shock registered on Wes's face. He lowered his brows and inclined his head closer as though he might not be hearing correctly. "What did you say?"

"We had a big party at Patrick and Clara's—in the barn. There was dancing and a lot of drinking. Hildy was so happy back then. She thought the sun rose and set on that man's shoulders."

Releasing her hold on Wes, she sat back on her heels. "We were just out of school—the both of us."

Listening intently, Wes ran a shaking hand through his hair.

"We danced together, Philo and I. And then later, I left alone to—visit the necessary." She looked at her hand and noticed blood on the handkerchief Wes had wrapped around her palm. "He surprised me on the way back. Pulled me off a ways…behind a toolshed."

As though he knew what was coming, Wes's gaze

shifted aside and he took a deep breath before looking back at her. He let her speak without interruption.

"I thought he was playing a prank. I think I laughed at first, but then I got anxious and tried to pull away. Philo kept trying to kiss me, and I wanted to leave, but he didn't let me go. He said…he said I'd wanted it the whole time. He told me a girl shouldn't behave as I did. around men, that I was just asking for trouble. He called me terrible names."

Her body trembled, but the words tumbled out, one after the other. "I think I tried to call out for help, but the music from the barn was loud, and he was heavy, pushing himself on me until I couldn't breathe."

When Wes met her gaze again, his lean face was streaked with tears. "He attacked you."

She swallowed hard. "He didn't hit me, but he was so much stronger. Afterward, he told me it was my fault. That I'd been asking for it with the clothing I wore and the way I looked at him. He said I was just a little whore and that it would break Hildy's heart if she ever found out what I'd made him do."

Her tender, even-tempered husband swore inventively, calling Philo every vile name he could think of. He clenched his fists on his thighs. Mariah blinked at the venom he released.

"I could have told her," she reminded him. "I didn't."

"Of course you didn't!" His voice and his lowered eyebrows relayed his disgust. "You were just a young girl. You had a terrible experience, one that made you feel ashamed. You didn't want anyone to know. He forced himself on you." He paused, looked toward the ceiling as though composing himself, and then back at her. "He raped you, and then he made you believe it was your fault. There's a place reserved in hell for a man like that."

"But if I'd just been smarter," she argued. "If I hadn't been so stupid, I'd have told and none of the rest of this would have happened."

"Stop it," he ordered. "Even if you'd told, what if he'd been convincing enough about what had happened and you'd ended up married to him?"

"Hildy wouldn't be dying. Those babies wouldn't be dead right now."

It was plain that she wasn't listening. "*Your* baby might have died."

That got her attention. Mariah met his gaze and swallowed hard. She might have lost John James!

"You can't know what might have happened," he continued. "And you can't take the blame for anything he did. You did the best you could. You were scared and humiliated. What he did to you is an abomination."

Wes reached to guide her up from the floor. "And Hildy isn't dying. She woke up during the night and again this morning."

"Oh!" Mariah almost lost her balance, but caught herself and leaned on Wes. "Oh, thank God." Her chest shook with dry sobs of relief. Hildy was awake! "I have to go see her."

"You can go see her as soon as we've cleaned you up and you've eaten."

Turning, she took in the debris for the first time. "I'm sorry. I'll clean it up."

Gently he held her arm and guided her to the bed. "No, you won't."

Her chest ached with the weight of a new fear. "Can you still love me knowing the truth?"

"Mariah." He stroked her cheek with profound tenderness. "Nothing is going to change the way I feel about you. You're brave and good, and you love deeply, so you hurt deeply. This is the first time you've let yourself feel any of it. All that anger and fear has been bottled up inside you."

Without a doubt, she felt as though she'd dropped a burden she'd been carrying on her shoulders far too long.

"Of course I still love you." Wes sat on the bed and gestured for her to join him. She folded herself onto his lap and he held her, smoothing her wet hair, stroking her shoulder and back through her wrapper, until a peace settled over her and her mind cleared. At last the trembling in her body ceased.

"So you found yourself expecting a baby, and what did you do?" She loved the way his voice vibrated in his chest and rumbled against her side.

"I told my grandfather about the baby. But I didn't tell him about Philo. He assumed I'd gotten myself that way out of foolishness. He came up with the plan to say I was attending school in Chicago. And while I was gone, he asked his friend Otto to provide him with the name on a mailbox that was rarely used. Even then he was planning for a little baby he'd never seen to have a father. My grandfather meant well."

"Yes, he did."

"And it was easy for me to fall into the lie. It prevented questions and suspicions. And no one was ever the wiser. I liked it. I had a husband who was conveniently gone, and I never had to deal with another man after that."

"What about Philo? Didn't he ever ask you about the baby?"

"Never. He acted as though nothing had ever happened." She lifted her head and looked up at him. "And that was easy, too. Because the charade was never in question. I was able to pretend it never happened."

It was all Wes could do to contain his anger and remain calm and comforting. The driving urge to find that man and make him suffer wasn't going to be appeased. Philo had to be stopped. But Mariah had entrusted Wes with a monumental confidence. He wouldn't betray her trust.

"I don't think this is a good time to tell Hildy after what she's been through. But I'm going to have to tell the others," she said. "Uncle Patrick and Aunt Clara. My parents." Her voice broke. "But what about John James?" she asked and wept again. "I've lied to him. I can't bear for him to know. He loves you so much."

Wes couldn't see past that lie, either. But he had lied

to the boy, as well, and to everyone in Mariah's entire family who believed he was such a great fellow. He knew only a slim measure of the humiliation she was facing, however. Looking back, regret edged its way into his thinking.

"Would you really have done anything differently if you knew then what you know now? Maybe Hildy wouldn't have married Philo, but what would have become of John James?"

"Of course that's why I lied for so long," she replied. "So he wouldn't grow up knowing how he'd come into the world. But my shame played just as big a part in not wanting to tell. I suppose I could have told the truth and then gone away to raise him somewhere else."

"Neither one of you would be the same person if you'd done that." He considered all the times he'd been so grateful to think John James had grown up in a big, loving family. "I only made it more difficult for you," he said. "By coming here and upsetting your life. Both of your lives. And I probably provoked Philo, because he resents both of us and takes it out on Hildy."

"I'm not sorry you came," she told him. "I'm just sick about what's going to happen from here on out. But I'm going to tell the truth. Once and for all."

"I'll be right there with you," he promised.

She dressed, and he took her downstairs to the dining room for breakfast, slipping currency into the hand of a maid in the hallway as they passed.

After they'd eaten, he got the buggy. Nervous as she was about going into Hildy's room and saying what she had to say, Mariah's breakfast settled in her belly like a rock.

Her palms were damp and she dabbed her forehead with her hankie. "I suppose I should ask them to come out into the hall or maybe we could find a small room."

Wes reached over and gave her hand an encouraging squeeze. "Your family loves you."

Mariah nodded, but knowing that Hildy loved her—and trusted her—made this worse.

When they reached the hospital room, she thought for a moment that she might throw up. She took several deep breaths to fortify herself.

Clara and Ina sat with Hildy, and Mariah was relieved to see the women keeping her company, rather than Hildy's father and brother. The others would know eventually, but at least she didn't have to say this in their presence.

Hildy's face was still swollen and discolored, but her eyes were open and she raised the arm without the cast toward Mariah immediately.

Mariah hurried forward. She wished she could take Hildy in her arms, but she was afraid of hurting her. She grasped her hand and reached to touch a lock of her dark hair and smooth it over the pillow.

"I was too ashamed to tell anyone about what was happening," Hildy told her.

Mariah pursed her lips and nodded. "I know."

"He always says he's sorry and promises it won't happen again. If I was a better wife it wouldn't happen."

Mariah's eyes stung and anger clawed her insides like prickly heat. Hearing Hildy accept the blame shocked her into comparing her own behavior.

"He loves me," Hildy told her.

Mariah leaned back in incredulity. "You are *not* excusing him."

"What else can I do?" she asked. "I don't have a choice. He's my husband. He can be convincing, and the law will believe him over me."

"What?" Mariah asked in disbelief.

"Patrick went to the marshal's office," Clara confirmed. "The law doesn't want to get involved in a marital dispute. Philo hasn't broken any laws in the state of Colorado."

In disbelief, Mariah twisted on the edge of the bed to glance at Wes. His return gaze assured her of his confidence in her. Hildy wasn't to blame for being treated badly. If she believed that, she had to believe what Wes had tried to tell her, as well. Mariah wasn't to blame for what had happened to her, either.

If she didn't tell Hildy now, Philo could get away with this. She looked back at her cousin with determination lighting an indignant fire inside her. "His cruelty is *not* your fault, Hildy. He can't be allowed to continue to hurt people. He's dangerous. There's something you don't know. Revealing this will change everything, but that man is not going to get away with what he's done. I'm not going to let him control us any longer."

Hildy's wide hazel eyes studied her expectantly. And then her poor swollen lips curved into a smile that must have hurt. "You know a way to help me?"

Mariah's heart ached at the hope she heard in her cousin's voice. "What I have to say is going to hurt. I should have told you a long time ago, but I couldn't. He's done something that will get him punished."

"What is it?" Hildy asked.

"Do you want us to leave you two alone?" Aunt Clara asked.

"No," Mariah answered. "You have to hear this, too." And then, with her heart pounding and her voice shaking, Mariah unfolded the happenings of that night more than seven years ago. "I was too afraid and ashamed to tell anyone," she finished. "And so I've lied to everyone all these years."

Hildy didn't cry. She didn't say anything for a long time, while Clara and Ina blew their noses into their hankies and Wes offered Mariah a clean white kerchief to do the same.

"Telling the truth might have saved you from this," Mariah told Hildy. "But I don't know. He's good at placing the blame for his bad behavior on the other person. We were both so young. Hearing you take the blame by not being a good enough wife showed me how foolish I was to feel responsible for what happened to you. All I can do now is ask you to forgive me for not telling the truth."

"There's nothing to forgive," Hildy replied. "You loved me and didn't want to see me hurt. You're not to blame."

Mariah swiped tears from her cheek. "I've never cried so much, not even when that happened, as I have this week. I could have filled buckets by now."

"What should we do now?" Aunt Clara asked in a quivering voice.

Mariah shook her head. "I don't know. Uncle Patrick should know. And probably my parents, but…"

"At least you went to Chicago and found Wes," Hildy said. "That part turned out well."

Mariah lifted her gaze to Wes's. The time of reckoning had arrived. She could agree, nod her head and say it had been good fortune. Or she could tell the truth. She'd been buried under lies far too long. Lies led only to more lies, and it took more energy than she possessed to keep up with them forever.

"I was already pregnant when I went to Chicago. I went there to give birth to John James and return home with no one knowing."

With a groan, Hildy raised up on one elbow. "Philo is John James's father?"

"Yes," Mariah confessed.

Hildy blinked as though the action would help her focus her thoughts. "Does he know?"

"No. From the moment I returned, he pretended as though nothing had ever happened. I'm convinced he believes the story about me marrying Wes." Mariah gave each of them, her cousin and her two aunts, a stern look. "He can't ever know."

Clara got up and placed another pillow behind

Hildy to help her sit. She smoothed the covers over Hildy's legs.

Hildy's gaze lifted to Wes at the foot of the iron bed. "Who are you, then?"

# *Chapter Nineteen*

So Wes explained what he'd done after finding John James's letters.

Mariah's aunt Ina got up. "Then you two aren't actually even *married?*"

"We got married the morning before we found out what had happened to Hildy," Wes told her. "I love Mariah and John James, and I intend to be here for them."

"What does my father think of all this?" Ina asked, referring to Louis.

Mariah explained his part in it. Wes told them about the old man's confusion regarding Wes, and how he hadn't thought it wise to add this problem to his challenged thinking.

"I agree it's better not to tell him," Clara said. "But there are others who need to know about this so Philo can be dealt with. His crime isn't only against my Hildy now."

"A meeting is in order," Mariah decided. "But only Marc and Uncle Patrick and Papa," she said.

"Not everyone needs to know," Clara insisted quickly. "We have to protect John James. Philo is too dangerous."

Amazed and more than relieved that Hildy and her mother weren't holding her silent fear against her and that they were thinking of John James's welfare, Mariah accepted hugs from her aunts.

"I'll arrange something right away." Wes held Mariah briefly, kissed her and headed out.

By that evening, those who'd needed to know had been told. Mariah's father had been shocked, and he'd apologized to her for not protecting her.

"One of the many things I've come to see through this," she told him, "is that we need to stop blaming ourselves and put the responsibility squarely where it belongs. We are the ones wronged, Hildy and I—the whole family, and Philo is the one responsible."

"It's hard not to look at where I might have failed in all this," Friederick said. "But you're right."

He seemed to think things over for another moment, glancing once at Wes. "So Wesley is who and what he says he is. All those stories are true and he's on the level—except that you never laid eyes on him before your grandfather's birthday party."

"Exactly so," she answered.

"I don't think John James needs to know this," Friederick said.

"All I can do is hope and pray the information stays with us and he never learns the truth."

"That's what I want, too," Friederick said. "It's our priority to protect him."

Mariah reached for Wes's hand and he squeezed hers reassuringly. The burden she'd carried for so long could no longer weigh her down now that she had people to help her carry it. She knew a sense of freedom she hadn't experienced since she'd been a young girl. The situation wasn't over, but she was no longer alone with it.

Glad to be on an even footing with Friederick, Marc and Patrick, Wes joined them in perusing the gaming halls and saloons that evening. It was a relief that they knew the truth about him.

They had developed a pattern. So that they didn't stand out, only one went into the establishment while the others waited outside. After a thorough search of the place, that person returned and another entered to ask the bartender and other employees if they'd seen anyone matching Philo's description.

Wes and Friederick stood in the shadows outside a noisy saloon in a disreputable area of town. Patrick waited across the street and Marc exited the building and they gathered to hear the first good news they'd had.

"The barkeep told me there was a ruckus upstairs last night. One of their girls was hurt. The description sounded like Philo. Hard to be sure without her account."

"We need to find the girl and ask her," Friederick said. "If he was upstairs with her, she most likely saw his scar." He looked to Wes. "He got burned a couple years back when a boiler exploded. He has scars on his shoulder and chest."

"I'll go ask her whereabouts," Wes offered.

Inside, pungent smoke hung in the humid air. Stale sweat and cheap whiskey added to the acrid smell. Sand and grit crunched under the soles of his boots on the pitted wooden floor. The piano player pounded out a tinny melody in which every other measure offended the ear with a sour note.

Nobody was listening anyway. Men of all shapes and sizes played poker, most of them squinting through the haze of cigar smoke. Here and there, women in cheap bright-colored dresses sat on customers' laps or lounged against the bar.

One such female approached Wes. "Haven't seen you around here before, cowboy." She rested a finger on the front of his shirt. "Want to buy me a drink?"

He took a bill from his pocket and handed it to her. "Don't have time for a drink, ma'am. But I'd appreciate some information."

She looked at the money, smiled up at him and tucked it between her powdered breasts. "Anything you need, honey."

"I'm looking for a tall man, about my height, but he has a lot of muscle. Big chest. Reddish hair and burn scars on his shoulder and chest."

Recognition flickered in lackluster brown eyes outlined with black kohl. "Why are you lookin' for him?"

"He's been known to rough up women pretty badly. His wife is in the hospital right now."

Her hesitancy disappeared. "You out to catch him for it?"

"Yes, ma'am."

She straightened her shoulders and raised her chin a notch. "Ain't nobody called me ma'am in a long time."

He was wondering if he needed to produce more money, when she volunteered, "Sounds like the fella what was in here last night and the night before. Last night he hit Delores. I think he did more than that, but ain't any lawman gonna go after a man for pokin' a whore."

"He'll meet justice square on if I find him," Wes told her.

She glanced around. Nobody paid any attention to their conversation. "She didn't come to work tonight. She's next door. Room twelve. Second floor."

Wes thanked her and exited into the night air, where he drew an unsullied breath. Light spilled from the broad windows and doorway of the saloon, leaving nearby doorways and the entrance to the alley in shadows.

He found the other men waiting in the darkness around the corner of the saloon.

"The girl who got beat up is in there." Wes nodded to the brothel only a few feet away. "Delores."

"Let's two of us stay out here and two go in," Friederick said.

They agreed that was a wise plan. Before they'd decided who was going in, a man on horseback rode up and slid to the ground, looping the reins around the hitching post.

Marc gestured for them to follow him farther into the shadows. "That's Philo."

Wes turned and recognized the big man's burly form as he approached the front door of the bordello. Every instinct went on alert. He heard nothing else the men beside him said.

"Philo!" he moved out of the shadows and into the street.

Philo spun on his heel. Wes knew the moment the man recognized him. But Philo didn't make any effort to run. He stepped off the boardwalk and faced Wes. "Now why is Mariah's new play toy following me?"

"You can't get rid of me," Wes replied.

"You got a bone to pick, Mr. Storyteller?"

"Got some bones to break is more like it."

Philo laughed. "There's no law against a man having a little fun in the big city."

"There are moral laws against a man beating his wife until she's nearly dead," Wes replied.

Philo scoffed. "Tend to your own business."

The other men stepped into the light. Philo's surprise was evident in the way he glanced behind him and then toward his horse, but he squared his shoulders. "Brought the whole family, did you?"

"You're going to answer for what you did to Hildy,"

Patrick told him. "You're not getting away with any more bullying."

"I don't know what she told you, but she's a stupid little b—"

Marc started forward, but his father and uncle stopped him.

"What about Mariah?" Wes asked. "I suppose she was lying, too."

"Whatever she said, it's a lie. She came on to me like one of these two-bit whores." He jerked his thumb over his shoulder.

Now blind with rage, Wes charged forward, lunging his shoulder into Philo's belly and knocking the wind out of him. Philo staggered backward, wheezing, then straightened.

Wes went after him again, knuckles cracking against his jaw in a burst of white-hot fury.

Philo rallied his defenses, drew back and landed a punch to the chest that sent Wes flying onto his backside in the dirt. Though winded, he sucked in a breath and jumped up faster than lightning before going after the man with both fists.

Philo was broader and more muscled, but Wes had not only the stamina borne of trudging hundreds of miles in a frozen wilderness, but the advantage of righteous determination.

Wes didn't see the punch coming that sent pain rocketing through his jaw and set red stars spinning in his vision. He stood with his hands on his thighs and shook his head to clear it. Through the haze, he squinted to bring Philo back into focus. With a roar that would have frightened a grizzly into turning the other way, he charged at the man who'd made so many lives a living hell.

One of the others could have stepped in and over-powered Philo, but almost as though an unspoken treaty held them where they stood, they offered Wes the time and space he needed to avenge a wrong.

Philo captured him in a burly hold, pinning his arms, crushing air from his lungs. Using one leg, Wes drew back and kicked his opponent's foot out from under him, and together they struck the wooden step of the boardwalk.

Shouts sounded, Wes only dimly aware of the crowd that had gathered. No one tried to stop the fight; instead, each time a punishing blow landed, shouts of encouragement and cheers volleyed in the dark street. It was probably no novelty to see a fistfight in this part of town. In fact it was most likely looked upon as recreation.

Spurred by the recent memories of his wife's anguish, Wes determinedly grappled until he held the upper position. Grasping Philo by the shirtfront and an ear, he slammed his head against the step.

Philo lay stunned for a second, long enough for Wes to shove his fist into his face. He slammed his head against the wood again.

"Don't kill him." Marc bent to rest a cautioning hand on Wes's arm. "Wes."

Wes's vision cleared and Philo's face came into focus, his eyelid and lower lip bleeding.

"The law can handle it from here, son," Friederick said from above him.

Wes placed a hand on the ground to steady himself and rose to his feet. His chest heaved painfully. Sweat stung his eyes. He backed away.

The front door of the nearest building flew open and slammed against the exterior wall. A short, generously proportioned woman came out of the opening, her wild black hair cascading over her shoulders like a cape of riotous curls. She tossed back the tresses, and along the side of her face dark bruising was visible in the light pouring from the saloon windows. She wore a red satin dressing gown she hadn't bothered to close, and a tattered corset revealed her sizable breasts and thighs.

Laughter erupted from the men who'd poured from the saloon, but her expression showed no amusement.

"That's the no good son of a bitch what worked me over last night!" she accused with venomous indignation.

The crowd hushed.

"Ain't nobody treats Big Delores bad. Especially not a ugly ham face what *didn't pay!*"

That announcement elicited more snickers.

Philo had managed to get up on one knee, but was too unsteady to rise. His head lolled on his neck as though his spine was made of rubber. He swiped his sleeve across his bleeding face and planted a foot flat on the ground in an attempt to stand.

He never made it.

All laughter ended abruptly, alerting Wes.

He turned in time to see Delores raise her arm from the folds of red satin. She aimed the barrel of a pearl-handled Colt .45 without wavering, held the revolver steady and squeezed the trigger.

# *Chapter Twenty*

The sound volleyed off the buildings across the street.

Philo's body jerked with the impact. He listed to the side and the crowd gasped.

Delores fired another shot. A dark stain widened across the front of Philo's shirt, proof that another bullet had found its deadly mark.

Wes stood and watched as Philo landed in a motionless heap, one leg twisted beneath him, staring up at the night sky.

The acrid smell of gunpowder reached Wes's nostrils.

The night stood in silence for one stunned moment. No piano music, no voices, not even a dog or a cricket interrupted the shocking silence.

And then all at once voices buzzed from both sides of the street, and behind Wes a commotion broke out. A stocky fellow wearing suspenders over a stained shirt approached Philo where he lay. He pressed his fingers against Philo's throat before straightening. "Fella's dead."

Patrick turned and walked deliberately away from the scene.

Marc glanced at Wes. Friederick squinted at Wes's face. "You need some ice on that eye. Might need a couple stitches."

Wes took his handkerchief from his pocket and blotted his eye. When he looked down at the cloth, it was stained bright red. "Let's get a wagon for him first."

No one slept that night. Clara and Ina stayed with Hildy. The others who knew what had happened gathered in Friederick and Henrietta's room. Friederick took charge of making plans. They had to finish out their stay at the Exhibition in the next few days and then get back to running a brewery.

"Mariah, I think you and I should go home and get the plant back into normal production. We have new contracts to fulfill, and a couple of trips to make to work out the details with these new clients.

"The extra workers we brought in can help the rest of you pack up here and see that our equipment is shipped home." He looked at Wes. "I need Mariah, but I think you should stay here."

Wes met his wife's concerned gaze. He'd already been thinking the same thing. Another week or two would give his face and eye time to heal.

"There would be a lot more explaining to do if the

children—if John James saw you like that," her father continued. "They already have to learn that Philo met with an unfortunate accident."

"The marshal wasn't able to get an account from any of the witnesses," Patrick said. "Seems everybody turns a blind eye to the goings-on in that part of town, and no one even asked Friederick or me if we saw what happened. Wes was at the doctor's by the time the marshal arrived that night."

"Apparently getting shot in front of a whorehouse is a pretty common happening," Marc commented wryly.

Clara raised an eyebrow in her son's direction.

"Well?" He shrugged.

"We didn't see any need to fill in the law," Patrick said. "It wouldn't have made a difference in the outcome. Except…" He glanced from person to person. "Do any of you take issue with that woman not being called to some sort of justice for shooting him? I don't think the law would look too kindly on her."

None of them spoke up.

Mariah didn't care who the woman was or what she did. She'd suffered Philo's abuse. If he hadn't been stopped, he would have gone on hurting women. Her thoughts traveled to his parents, though. "What about the Ulrichs?" she asked. "They deserve to know the truth about his death, don't they?"

Patrick nodded. "A couple of us will talk to them when we take his body home. I'm pretty sure they won't want the details of his death to become public."

"Will you tell them about Hildy, too?"

"I'll leave that up to her," her uncle answered.

And so it came about that Wes kissed Mariah goodbye at the train station the next day. She pressed her hand against the window glass as the passenger car pulled away from the depot. Wes grew smaller and smaller as the train chugged away from Denver.

Being separated from him was as painful, and yet different, than being apart from her son. She felt as though she was going to be incomplete until Wes had finished in Denver and headed home.

Home. The big house outside Ruby Creek had come to be their home. Her grandfather had suggested a move before, but for the first time, she let herself think about his suggestion of getting their own place. Only now a move wouldn't be so that no one saw them sleeping separately. Now a house would be a place where they could have a honeymoon of sorts and make it their own home.

The idea took on more merit the longer she considered it. Mariah wasn't used to inactivity or to not having John James with her. She'd been missing him terribly, though she was grateful he'd been staying safely away from all that had transpired.

The rocking motion of the train lulled her into sleepiness, and she dozed off and on. Sleep hadn't come easily for quite some time. A tumble of thoughts still whirled in her head, with disturbing images and snips of conversation rousing her every so often. Every time an image of Philo arose in her head, she got a tight, panicky feeling and roused awake.

Philo was dead, of course. She'd heard the accounts from the men who were right there when he'd been shot. But she hadn't seen him die, nor had she seen his body, so there was still an unreality to the fact. Her mind wouldn't release images of Philo's cruelty to Hildy. And now that the memories had been released, tormenting images from that night years ago came into focus as clearly as if they'd just happened.

She'd made Wes tell her what had happened in front of the bordello at least half a dozen times. She'd even wanted to go talk to the woman who'd shot him, but Wes had discouraged her. What good would it do? None, she'd agreed.

She'd never laid eyes on the woman. She had no idea what kind of a life had led her to where she'd been the first time Philo crossed her path. Certainly she wasn't working in that place by choice.

Mariah opened her eyes and sat up. Beside her, her mother rested with her eyes closed. Instinctively she reached over and groped for Mariah's hand. "You're not sleeping well?"

"No."

Henrietta gently squeezed her fingers. "I knew something changed the year that Hildy got married. If only I'd known. I wish I could have helped you. This was a terrible thing for a mother to learn after the fact. I feel that I've let you down."

"We all have something to live with, Mama. But I know how useless it is to blame yourself for things you can't control."

"Just because I'm blind doesn't mean I can't see people," her mother said. "I sensed something about Philo, but I never understood the reason for my unease with him. I should have known Hildy was hiding something. She always spent as much time with me as she did at her own place, so I knew she wasn't happy. I just didn't know the extent of what the poor girl was going through."

Mariah patted her hand and described some of the landscape to her mother. "There are moose on a flat spot of land with a ridge overhead. Three of them. Two have big antlers. Oh, and there's a young one that just stepped from behind some bushes."

"What does the sky look like?"

"It's clear today. I can't see a cloud anywhere. Mama, why do you think women become prostitutes?"

"Maybe because they don't have other choices."

Mariah leaned her head back against the upholstered seat. "Last night I thought about what a different person I'd have been if I didn't have a family. I couldn't help questioning what it must be like to grow up without people who care about you."

"Your Wes would know about that now, wouldn't he?"

Mariah turned her head to look at her mother. "You know about his childhood?"

Henrietta's lips curved up. "He talks to me."

Mariah brought her mother's fingers up to her face to feel her smile. "He thinks the world of you and Father."

"He thinks the universe of you."

"Yes, he does." She thought a minute. "When we get home I'm going to send a telegram and wire money to Father. I want that woman to have another choice. He'll take it for me."

"It's good to recognize how fortunate we are. If you're moved to do this for that woman, then you should do it."

Mariah closed her eyes. This time she slept for a few restful hours.

Mariah threw herself into seeing after John James's needs and squaring away her duties at the brewery. Sleep was still a hard-to-come-by commodity. She missed Wes terribly and lay awake long into the dark hours each night.

News came to them that the Ulrichs had quietly buried Philo on their land. Mariah dreamed about him that night and woke in a cold sweat, a sick feeling in her stomach.

Friederick asked if she was up to traveling to the western part of the state. A hotel located at a hot springs had signed a contract, and he and Louis agreed that a personal visit would be good business and in their best interests.

Mariah approved and took John James with her. She appreciated time alone with him. Perhaps her father had even been thinking she needed this time with her son.

Walking along the main street in the picturesque town in the foothills, she felt like a different person. Not only was she dressed in a smart two-piece velvet-trimmed blue dress she'd never dreamed she would feel comfortable wearing, but she was truly, without deception, a married woman. She looked down at the ring on her left hand and a swift pang of loneliness swept over her. She missed him. She missed her husband.

A horse and rider passed, and John James turned to watch the man and his mount. Her son had lost his baby fat, and the curve of his cheek along with the way he squinted against the sunlight under the bill of his cap sharply reminded Mariah of the man she'd despised so intently.

The thought stabbed her with fear.

Why now? Why this way?

She looked away, and then back at John James, scrutinizing his features for a keener resemblance. He had her hair color and her blue eyes, didn't he?

John James had always been her boy and her boy alone. Her mind had never allowed her to connect him in any way with the man she couldn't bear to look at or think of. But the connection had been made the day she'd admitted to herself and to others that Philo was her son's father. It had been so much easier to fool herself and to pretend he had an absent father.

Now the truth had been planted. The facts were alive and thriving. Her parents knew. Hildy knew. Wes knew. This person she treasured and adored, this little human being she'd brought into the world, nurtured and protected…her boy had been fathered by a monster.

Panic fluttered in her chest. She pressed a hand against the front of her jacket and took a calming breath. Nothing had changed. He was still the same sweet, precious, innocent child he'd always been.

"I'm gonna ask Papa to teach me to ride a horse like that."

Her eyes filled with tears. Wes was his father now. "He would love to teach you to ride."

Something in her voice must have alerted him to her distress. He glanced up. "Why are you sad?"

"I'm not sad. I'm proud, thinking about what a fine man you're going to grow up to be."

"Just like Papa."

"Yes," she managed. "Just like him."

But she couldn't escape the nagging trepidation that threatened her peace of mind. Working at the brewery was often a tedious job. Having family members underfoot and beside you at work and at home could be smothering if a person wasn't used to it. Wes had spent his life sailing from one glorious adventure to the next. She could hardly believe that what she had to offer would be a more stimulating and fulfilling existence.

Besides, he knew the whole truth about her now, the unvarnished truth about John James. After he'd had time to take it all in, would John James's conception make a difference in how Wes perceived her?

Now that Mariah had stopped pretending, a myriad

of concerns kept her head reeling. She may be dressed differently but she was no longer projecting the image of a confident, proud and opinionated woman. Now she was plain, old, ordinary Mariah. The strength she'd prided herself on for so long had dissolved.

If Wes moved on now, she'd have nothing to fall back on.

# Chapter Twenty-One

The remainder of the family returned to Ruby Creek the following week. As family members got down from the wagon, Mariah caught sight of Wes, and her heart lurched. With his hat clutched in his hand and the sun pouring over his dark hair and broad shoulders, he looked so good, she could scarcely catch her breath. He spotted her and started forward. His gait was more even than it had been when he'd first come to Colorado. His leg had gradually been healing.

"Wes is barely limping at all," she said to her mother beside her.

"Is your father heading this way?" Mama asked.

Mariah turned to catch the expectant joy on her mother's face, and the sight warmed her heart. "He's looking at you, Mama."

She turned her attention back to the men crossing the front lawn. She wished she'd been uninhibited enough

to run toward him as John James had done. Her son
reached him and Wes swept up John James into a hug
and kissed his cheeks.

Mariah hurried forward then, and Wes set down John
James to enfold her in his strong arms and kiss her
soundly. He had a pinkish scar at the corner of his eye,
but he'd never looked better.

"I've missed you," he said.

She'd needed to hear those words. "I've missed you,
too."

Tail wagging, Yuri waited obediently at Wes's feet
until Wes released Mariah and bent to give the dog's
head a pat and scratch his ears.

"I took good care of him for you," John James
assured him.

"He looks fatter than when I left."

John James giggled. "He likes Grandmama's
dumplings."

"When did you feed him dumplings?" Mariah
asked, but her chiding didn't hold any merit, because
Wes laughed.

"Felix, you've grown into your feet," he said to the
other dog that was no longer puppy-size. The furry
younger dog wedged its way in between Yuri and Wes,
vying for attention. He wagged his tail so hard his entire
rear end swayed back and forth.

"Mama lets Yuri sleep with me and Felix now," John
James told him.

Wes tilted his head. "He'll never want to sleep in the
snow again, will he?"

"He don't have to sleep outside anymore," John James told him matter-of-factly. "Now that you're home, he can sleep with you and Mama."

Wes straightened and grinned at her. "How would you like that, Mama?"

"We'll have to talk about it," she replied with one brow raised. Her thoughts weren't on the dog, however, but on the fact that Wes would once again be sharing her room that night.

"We're going to have a celebration this evening!" Henrietta announced. Arm in arm with Wes, Mariah turned to see her parents standing in a similar embrace. "We'll celebrate the success of our presence at the Exposition," her mother continued. "And we will toast to new beginnings."

Hildy made her way across the grass with Clara at her side. The plaster cast was still on her arm, suspended by a sling around her neck, but she walked steadily and had a smile for John James.

"Mama told me about the accident," he said, running up and stopping in front of her. "Is your arm better yet?"

"It doesn't hurt much." She managed to bend down and let him hug her around the neck. She smiled and straightened.

Louis approached and greeted Hildy with a hug.

"Ladies, we have work to do!" Henrietta called.

Mariah reluctantly separated herself from Wes and followed the women into the house. The mouthwatering smells of *kartoffelsalat,* a salad made from marinated boiled potatoes and smoked *steckerlfisch* already filled the kitchen.

Henrietta assigned Mariah the task of slicing sausages and cheese, while Hildy was ushered into a comfortable chair to watch the activity.

"It's so good to be home," Hildy said.

"What will you do now?" Mary Violet asked, pausing with a steaming bowl of poppy seed–studded noodles in her hands. "Will you want to stay in your house alone?"

A hush fell over the kitchen. Hildy looked from Mariah to the other women. "Have all of you learned what Philo did to me?" she asked.

"I told them," Clara said. "I thought it would be best if they knew, and this way they can help you."

"It's best, Mama," Hildy told her with a nod. "I'm just embarrassed."

"Don't be ashamed," Henrietta said sternly from where she sat on a stool at the center workspace. She got to her feet and unerringly made her way to Hildy, palm extended.

Hildy reached for her hand, and Henrietta moved close to lay a palm alongside her niece's cheek. "You are not the one who holds responsibility for wrongdoing. Hold your head high. You survived. And you are going to be stronger than ever."

The others murmured their agreement.

When Henrietta turned to go back to her stool, Mariah knew that if her mother had been able to see, she would have looked at Mariah to give her the same assurance.

"I don't want to be alone now," Hildy said. "I need my family around me."

"You can come home," Clara assured her.

"Or you can share my room," Mariah's sister Sylvie suggested.

"It's good to be welcome," Hildy said with a smile and a nod. Then she waved with a dismissive gesture that included each of them. "And don't treat me with sympathy. I might look bad right now, but I'm tougher than I look, and I'll be better than before."

The other females turned back to their tasks and conversations resumed. The two tall windows were raised, and a refreshing gust of cooler air blew in from the outside.

Blotting tears with the hem of her apron, Mariah crossed to Hildy's side. Hildy reached for her hand, stood and drew her into the pantry, where the pungent scents of brine and sauerkraut surrounded them.

"I'm so proud of you," Mariah told her with heartfelt sincerity. "And I love you very much."

"I'm proud of you, too," she said softly, even though they were alone in the enclosed space. "Thank you for what you did. Speaking up like that. I knew then that if you could be brave, I could, too."

Mariah told her about the Ulrichs' desire to keep the account of Philo's death silent and how they'd buried him without a service.

Hildy nodded thoughtfully. "Maybe someday I'll go there, but not for a long time."

They moved to the doorway and Mariah gave her cousin's hand a squeeze. At last the food was served, and the family gathered in the dining hall, spilling over into the great room.

"Good health to the Spanglers!" Henrietta cried.

A cheer rose, and lines formed before the food tables.

Mariah stood with John James in front of her and Wes behind, his arms encircling her. She closed her eyes, remembering the times she'd stood in this very spot and yearned for a love such as the one Wes had offered her.

Henrietta called her name.

"Here, Mama."

"Fix your grandfather a plate, will you, please? He's tired this evening. He likes the cabbage."

Mariah prepared a plate for Louis and carried it to the great room where he sat in his chair, the mountain hounds lounging at his feet. They raised their heads and sniffed the air at her approach. "Here's a plate for you."

"Thank you, dear."

She transferred the plate and fork to his hands. "Wes and I will come and sit near you."

Once they had their plates, they pulled footstools close to Louis and sat. After everyone had eaten and refilled their mugs of beer, Louis raised a hand to gain their attention. "Everyone gather in here."

It took several minutes to round up those from the kitchen and dining hall, but eventually everyone had been seated or leaned in a doorway.

"Friederick and I have been talking things over the past couple of days," Louis began. "Patrick's been at the table, too, of course. I trust this won't come as a shock to any of you. I've decided it's time I take leave of my position and hand down the work to these capable fellows. They've been doing almost everything anyhow, so it won't be much of a change for them."

Mariah looked at her father, and he gave her a nod of assurance. She'd known that one day her grandfather would step away from the brewery, but to her he *was* Spangler Brewery.

An overwhelming sadness gripped her at Louis's decision. He'd been in charge of things for as long as she could remember. It was painful to recognize he was no longer capable, but he'd always known what was best for the company. Even now, when his memory was slipping—and maybe he recognized the fact and it concerned him—but even now he was thinking of the welfare of the brewery that his father and uncles had started when they'd come to this country.

Louis sought her face in the crowd and winked.

She smiled through a blur of tears. As difficult as it was to imagine the brewery without him present, he deserved to enjoy spending his days taking it easy.

"And now..." Louis glanced toward Friederick. "Now address the opening at the mash house."

The mash house. Philo's position as supervisor. Mariah glanced at Hildy. Her cousin was listening with interest.

Friederick stood holding a half-full mug of beer. "Arlen will be taking over that position." He gestured toward his son with the mug. "Arlen learned the process a couple of years ago. He's more than capable of overseeing the tanks and grist cases."

Arlen nodded and glanced at his family members with a combination of embarrassment and pride.

Friederick continued, "He's been working the mash machines, and he took over the building while the rest of us were in Denver." He nodded at Arlen. "And a fine job you did, son."

Mariah's brother received the praise with a satisfied grin. Dutch slapped him on the back, causing his beer to slosh in the mug.

Friederick moved to stand beside his father-in-law's chair. "That leaves Arlen's position open."

He had everyone's attention again.

"Now we've talked it over and concluded that over the past several weeks Wesley has proved himself. We agree that he has a head for learning the business."

Several appreciative murmurs rippled through the gathering, and all eyes turned to Wes.

Wes's surprise appeared as genuine as the jolt Mariah experienced at hearing his name. His eyebrows climbed his forehead.

"So, Wesley," Friederick continued. "You're hereby promoted to supervising maintenance of the grist mills and mash tanks. Arlen will travel between both jobs for a while until he's sure you've got the hang of it, so you won't be set to the task without all the guidance you need to feel confident."

Wes didn't appear to have any words. He blinked and glanced from her father to Mariah and back. Unexpectedly she found herself holding her breath to see what he would say. A niggle of fear squirmed in her belly while she waited.

If he intended to cut and run, there wouldn't be a better time than this to make the break.

"It's one of the most physically demanding jobs at the brewery," Friederick said. "Not one that every man could handle. But I'm convinced you're cut out for the work. Unless you don't want the job."

Mariah still hadn't breathed, and now she got butterflies in her stomach as though she stood perched on the edge of a cliff, ready to jump.

"Oh, I want the position, sir," Wes told him, and then shook his head as though to clear his thoughts.

Mariah released a breath.

Wes tilted his head in a questioning gesture. "I'm just…well, I'm overwhelmed by your confidence."

"If Mariah trusts you, I trust you," Friederick replied.

That remark garnered a couple of laughs, and Gerd slapped Wes on the back.

Family members congratulated both Arlen and Wes. Her husband strode close to give Mariah a brief hug. Conversation teemed around them.

"Did you know anything about this?" he asked.

She shook her head. "I had no idea."

"I guess I'm officially a part of the family now," he said.

She agreed with a nod. "You are."

Roth came over to shake Wes's hand and challenge him to a playful competition as to who could carry the heaviest machinery. At the younger man's continued teasing, Wes's good-natured laugh filled the room.

Mariah's mother found Wes and took his hand, leading him toward the dessert table. Mariah hung back and observed as Wes lowered his head to listen to something she said, and she rested her hand on his arm.

He had accepted the job, and he seemed pleased as punch about it. From the very first night he'd arrived here, her family had absorbed him into their midst, and it was plain this acceptance was what Wes had always wanted. He'd said as much on various occasions. He'd come here to make an impact on John James's life, but in the meantime he'd found the family he'd never had.

He was good to her, Mariah couldn't deny it. And she adored him. But was it her he truly loved? Or was his true love the family he craved, and she just happened to come along with the appealing package? Hard as she tried, she couldn't think of a single reason why he'd choose her over any other woman, except that she was John James's mother and a Spangler.

If she didn't have this family or a son, would she hold the same charm?

Around her, conversation swelled and someone spoke

to her. After replying distractedly, she picked up several empty serving bowls and carried them to the kitchen.

Sometime later, Friederick came and whisked Henrietta from her duties. "You can do without her for the rest of the evening," he declared with a smile. "I've missed my wife."

"I'm going home with my parents tonight," Hildy told Mariah. "But I think I'll accept Sylvie's offer to stay here with her for a while. The activity and company will keep me busy."

"You know we love having you here," Mariah assured her.

Annika touched Hildy's shoulder. "You should probably go home and rest. You had a long trip today, and you must be tired." She turned to Mariah. "And you follow Mama's example and go off with your husband. We will finish here."

Mariah dried her hands and wished them a goodnight. She located Wes and John James outside with other fathers and children who were playing fetch with the dogs in the moonlight.

"Let's go get you ready for bed," she called to her boy. "He needs a bath now."

"I can bathe him," Wes said.

"I'll do it. You come in whenever you're ready."

"I'm ready now."

She ended up sitting on a stool while he helped John James wash his hair and lather his body, then rinse. John James wanted to dry himself.

Once he was tucked into bed and given kisses, John James patted the mattress and Felix jumped up to join him. "Yuri can sleep with you and Mama if you want."

Panting, the big dog looked up at Wes.

"I think he needs to stay outside at night," Wes answered.

"But he'll be lonely."

"Then he can sleep with you," Wes told him. "Your mama and I don't need his company."

It took some coaxing to get the animal to stop following Wes and stay in the room with John James, but eventually, he plopped down on the rug beside the bed.

Wes followed Mariah to their room, where they each lit a lamp. He'd missed her so much and had counted the days and the hours until he was back here with her. She looked so pretty, her skin flushed from the warm night and her chores. Around her face, little tendrils of her shiny pale hair glowed in the lamplight once she had it lit.

He locked the door.

She didn't meet his eyes.

"Are you angry that I let Yuri sleep in the house?" she asked.

"No." He grinned. "I just didn't want him sleeping with us. We're newlyweds."

She hurried to the bureau and took out a folded nightdress, then carried it behind the dressing screen.

Disappointment carved a notch in his plans. He hadn't imagined her undressing herself behind that cussed screen. "Are you angry with me about something?"

"No."

He used the jack to remove his boots and stood them beside the bureau. Water splashed and he pictured her washing. All right, she probably needed privacy for her nighttime ablutions.

He removed his shirt and tossed it into the woven basket beside a chest. "Is it all right with you that I got the promotion in the mash house?"

She stepped from behind the screen dressed in the white cotton nightdress. "Of course," she said. "I trust their judgment. And you deserved the job."

Something didn't feel right. This wasn't the same easy conversation they'd shared in Denver. He had a sorry feeling that he was the only one who'd been looking forward to being alone tonight. "What's bothering you?"

She sat at her dressing table and took the pins from her hair. "What makes you think something's bothering me?"

"Because you haven't looked at me since we came into this room."

She raised her hairbrush. "It's nothing."

Wesley stepped up behind her and took the brush from her hand. "If it's a concern to you, it's something to me. Has something happened that I don't know about? Have I made a mistake or overlooked anything?"

Mariah shook her head, but she didn't meet his eyes in the mirror.

He stood studying her reflection. He loved everything about this woman, except her stubborn refusal to open up. Glancing at the hairbrush in his hand, he applied it to her hair and ran the bristles through the golden waves from her scalp to the ends. He repeated the action.

He remembered the day he'd washed her hair and bathed her. He recalled the night they'd made love in the hotel room, and the morning he'd awakened beside her. His need for this woman was an ache he was learning to enjoy, and one that would never be easily appeased. He wasn't going to let anything spoil what he knew they could have.

Setting down the brush, he lowered his face to inhale the scent of her fragrant hair. He nuzzled her jaw and caressed her neck and shoulders.

Her eyelids fluttered down.

When she raised them again, he met and held her blue gaze in the mirror. "I love you, Mariah."

The swift sheen of tears caught him by surprise, but she answered, "I love you."

She turned and looked up, and he bent at the waist to cover her lips in a gentle hello. *I've missed you,* the kiss whispered. *I've thought of this moment every day and every night.*

She rested her fingers against his jaw, and that innocent touch shot a torrent of desire throughout his body. He groaned against her mouth and kissed her more deeply.

Mariah twisted on the bench until she faced him and raised her arms to circle his neck. Wes slid his palm across her shoulder and down to the swell of her breast, where he caressed her nipple into a tight bud. She inched away from the kiss and her breath came in short gasps. With her eyes closed, she trembled under his touch.

He raised his left hand to her other breast, and she let her head fall back.

"Come lie with me," he urged, taking her hand to guide her from the seat. She helped him gather the fabric of her garment and pull it over her head, exposing the enticing sight of her curves and hollows. "You are more beautiful than I remembered."

"Truly?"

"Without a doubt." He leaned on one elbow so he could admire her in the lamplight. She returned his kisses, but there was a sadness about her passion he wished he could identify and abolish. "What pleases you, Mariah?" he asked against her mouth.

"Everything about this pleases me," she replied.

"You like it when I touch you here?"

"Ye-es."

"And here?"

Her soft gasp was his response.

"I've missed you," he said.

"Wes?" His softly spoken name was a question.

He looked into her beseeching blue eyes. "What?"

"Would you still be happy if we got a place of our own?" she asked. "Like my grandfather suggested?"

His reaction took longer than it would have had he not

been focused on the pleasure he got from her reactions to his caresses. He moved his weight to his elbow again. "He suggested that so we could have separate rooms." He frowned. "You want to sleep in separate rooms?"

She clutched his shoulder tightly. "No, of course not."

"Well." He focused on a reply to her question. "Then I suppose I'd like to live in our own home."

"And what if I cooked for you?"

He frowned at her this time. "Is this a warning of some sort?"

"I'm actually an adequate cook."

"Remember I survived entire winters on hardtack and fish," he told her and lowered his lips for another kiss.

She interrupted it a minute later. "It would be just us then. Just the three of us. We might only come here for holidays."

Wes dropped his head until his chin touched his chest. Her questions were frustrating.

"Would you still be happy?" she asked. "Would you still want to stay?"

Like a jagged streak of lightning illuminating a midnight sky, her questions awakened a perfectly clear realization. He sat up and looked down at her, with golden hair spread across the bedclothes and doubt shading uncertain eyes. "What is it you're really asking me, Mariah? What fear is keeping you so distant? It wasn't between us like this the last time we were together. Have I done something to make you question my sincerity? Why are you doubting my love for you?"

Tears welled in her eyes and spilled over. Reaching for the sheet, she sat and covered herself, tucking the sheet under her arms.

"Say it," he said, rather sternly this time. "You're my wife now, Mariah. I've pledged to love you and care for you. You can't keep all your thoughts and concerns to yourself any longer. Not like you've always done. Like you did for years. It's unfair."

And it was unfair, Mariah thought, as a sweeping realization rocked her thinking once again. He had promised to love her and care for her. He'd made those vows of his own accord. "I'm afraid," she whispered. "Afraid I'm not what you want or need. Afraid you'll grow bored with me and this simple life and move on to somewhere more exciting."

He raised a hand in exasperation. "And what have I ever done to make you question me?"

She shook her head, because he'd done nothing. Her fears were all in her own mind. "From the first, I was afraid you'd make John James love you and then leave. I didn't know I would come to rely on you. I never expected to depend on you. I didn't know I was going to love you so much that the thought of losing you would be a cavernous ache inside."

She brought a balled fist to her breast.

"I have nothing more than my word to offer you," he said. "And my devotion." He reached for her hand, uncurling her fingers and raising them to his lips, where he kissed the backs. He tucked back an unruly tress of her hair. "No one has ever cared whether I stayed or left." His voice was uncommonly gruff, and she suspected emotion had changed its timbre.

"I've never had a home or a family, never been a son or a brother, let alone a husband. You're the one who's going to find me tedious, because I love being here. I love being with you and spending my days and nights with you and John James, and that's not going to change. You'll be begging me to take my leave so you can spend a few hours in privacy."

She shook her head. "I've been alone," she said. "Right in the middle of this big, loud family, I was alone with my fear and shame…until you came."

"I'll live anywhere as long as you and John James are there," he assured her. "I love your family, Mariah. They are the parents and brothers and sisters I never had. But I'm in love with *you*. And I'll be content wherever you want to be. As long as you always tell me what you're thinking and feeling. And as long as you let me love you."

Mariah lunged forward to wrap her arms around his neck and hug him hard. His arms curled around her back, with one hand splayed against her spine, pressing her to him.

"I never thanked you for understanding," she said against his warm neck. "Thank you for sticking with me, even when I was awful."

"You were never awful. You were afraid. And hurting. You didn't know me or what I could do to you and John James. I bullied my way into your life. You were like a mother bear looking out for her cub. I'm glad I didn't think it all through before I came barging in here, because I wouldn't have found you if I had."

He cupped her head between his hands and pulled her away so he could look into her face. "Promise you won't doubt me again. You won't doubt my love or my commitment. *Our* commitment."

Mariah couldn't help the tears that blurred her vision and spilled over. "You stuck with me through the wo-orst." The last word broke, but she composed herself because she needed to assure him. The love and concern and respect she saw in his eyes settled all the misgivings that had tried to assail her. "I *was* awful, but you loved me anyway. How can you resist me if I'm kind and generous?"

She smiled despite the ache, because she loved him so fiercely and reassuring him meant everything.

"I can't resist you. And I don't want to."

She raised her lips to his and his kiss promised more than even his words. When she was breathless from the beauty and wonder of his caresses, once he'd lowered her back to the mattress and they lay facing each other, she skimmed his jaw and placed her fingers on his warm, damp lips. "Thank you for loving me."

He grinned. "You should be thanking John James. He wrote the letters that got me here."

"I'll thank him tomorrow. Tonight is all ours."

"Peculiar, really," he said. "How old Otto died but a few months before I got my leg busted up in that trap.

Those letters were waiting for me when I got to Juneau City. The new postmaster brought them to me while I was lying in my bunk and left the wrapped bundle on the crate beside me. I didn't look at them for weeks, but once I read one, I read them all.

"I'd been feeling pretty sorry for myself. Pretty lonesome. Wondering if it wouldn't've been better if the infection hadn't just run its course and left me dead."

Mariah kissed his chin. "Thank God it didn't."

"John James's letters dredged up feelings I'd buried years before. Questions about why my parents hadn't wanted me or found a decent home for me. When I read how much he needed his father to want him, I couldn't think of anything else but making that happen. It was purely selfish."

"It was purely *un*selfish," she disagreed. She pushed up then, away from him, and stood. He gazed upon her loveliness, and she smiled, knowing the effect she had on him and enjoying it.

She moved away and lowered the wicks in both the lamps before returning to kneel on the bed beside him. "Do you think we might finish our conversation another time?"

"We have a lifetime," he promised and reached to draw her down beside him.

The only words that followed were softly murmured endearments. Wes was no longer her make-believe husband, but her husband in spirit and body for the rest of their lives.

*Bestselling author Lynne Graham is back
with a fabulous new trilogy!*

## PREGNANT BRIDES

*Three ordinary girls—naive, but also honest and plucky…*

*Three fabulously wealthy, impossibly handsome
and very ruthless men…*

*When opposites attract and passion leads to pregnancy…
it can only mean marriage!*

*Available next month from Harlequin Presents®:
the first installment*

# DESERT PRINCE, BRIDE OF INNOCENCE

\* \* \*

'THIS EVENING I'm flying to New York for two weeks,'
Jasim imparted with a casualness that made her heart sink
like a stone. 'That's why I had you brought here. I own this
apartment and you'll be comfortable here while I'm abroad.'

'I can afford my own accommodation although I may not
need it for long. I'll have another job by the time you
get back—'

Jasim released a slightly harsh laugh. 'There's no need for
you to look for another position. How would I ever see you?
Don't you understand what I'm offering you?'

Elinor stood very still. 'No, I must be incredibly thick
because I haven't quite worked out yet what you're offering
me.…'

His charismatic smile slashed his lean dark visage.
'Naturally, I want to take care of you.…'

HPEX0110A

'No, thanks.' Elinor forced a smile and mentally willed him not to demean her with some sordid proposition. 'The only man who will ever take *care* of me with my agreement will be my husband. I'm willing to wait for you to come bac but I'm not willing to be kept by you. I'm a very independe woman and what I give, I give freely.'

Jasim frowned. 'You make it all sound so serious.'

'What happened between us last night left pure chaos in its wake. Right now, I don't know whether I'm on my head my heels. I'll stay for a while because I have nowhere else t go in the short term. So maybe it's good that you'll be away for a while.'

Jasim pulled out his wallet to extract a card. 'My private number,' he told her, presenting her with it as though it was precious gift, which indeed it was. Many women would hav done just about anything to gain access to that direct hotline to him, but his staff guarded his privacy with scrupulous car

Before he could close the wallet, his blood ran cold in hi veins. How could he have made such a serious oversight? What if he had got her pregnant? He knew that an unplanne pregnancy would engulf his life like an avalanche, crush his freedom and suffocate him. He barely stilled a shudder at th threat of such an outcome and thought how ironic it was tha what his older brother had longed and prayed for to secure th line to the throne should strike Jasim as an absolute disaster...

\* \* \*

*What will proud Prince Jasim do if Elinor is expecting his roya baby? Perhaps an arranged marriage is the only solution! But will Elinor agree? Find out in DESERT PRINCE, BRIDE OF INNOCENCE by Lynne Graham [#2884], available from Harlequin Presents® in January 2010.*

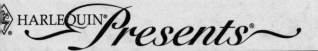

# HARLEQUIN Presents

## AT HIS *Service*

### *From glass slippers to silk sheets*

Once upon a time there was a humble housekeeper.
Proud but poor, she went to work for a charming and
ruthless rich man!

She thought her place was below stairs—
but her gorgeous boss had other ideas.

Her place was in the bedroom, between his
luxurious silk sheets.

Stripped of her threadbare uniform, buxom and blushing
in his bed, she'll discover that a woman's work has never
been so much fun!

Look out for:

## POWERFUL ITALIAN, PENNILESS HOUSEKEEPER

*by India Grey*

#2886

*Available January 2010*

**www.eHarlequin.com**

## New Year, New Man!

*For the perfect New Year's punch,*
*blend the following:*

- *One woman determined to find her inner vixen*
- *A notorious—and notoriously hot!—playboy*
- *A provocative New Year's Eve bash*
- *An impulsive kiss that leads to a night of explosive passion!*

When the clock hits midnight Claire Daniels
kisses the guy standing closest to her, but
the kiss doesn't end after the bells stop ringing....

**Look for**

# Moonstruck

**by *USA TODAY* bestselling author**

# JULIE KENNER

*Available January*

---

# red-hot reads

www.eHarlequin.com

Welcome to Montana—the home of bold men and
daring women, where tales of passion, adventure
and intrigue unfold beneath the Big Sky.

*Rogue Stallion* by DIANA PALMER

Undaunted by rogue cop Sterling McCallum's heart of
stone and his warnings to back off, Jessica Larson stands
her ground, braving the rising emotions between them
until the mystery of his past comes to the surface.

*Montana* ★ MAVERICKS™

**RETURN TO BIG SKY COUNTRY**

*Available in January 2010 wherever you buy books.*

# REQUEST YOUR FREE BOOKS!

 **Harlequin® Historical**
Historical Romantic Adventure!

## 2 FREE NOVELS PLUS 2 FREE GIFTS!

**YES!** Please send me 2 FREE Harlequin® Historical novels and my 2 FREE gifts (gifts are worth about $10). After receiving them, if I don't wish to receive any more books, I can return the shipping statement marked "cancel". If I don't cancel, I will receive 6 brand-new novels every month and be billed just $4.94 per book in the U.S. or $5.49 per book in Canada. That's a savings of 20% off the cover price! It's quite a bargain! Shipping and handling is just 50¢ per book.* I understand that accepting the 2 free books and gifts places me under no obligation to buy anything. I can always return a shipment and cancel at any time. Even if I never buy another book, the two free books and gifts are mine to keep forever.

246 HDN EYS3   349 HDN EYTF

| | | |
|---|---|---|
| Name | (PLEASE PRINT) | |
| Address | | Apt. # |
| City | State/Prov. | Zip/Postal Code |

Signature (if under 18, a parent or guardian must sign)

### Mail to the Harlequin Reader Service:
**IN U.S.A.:** P.O. Box 1867, Buffalo, NY  14240-1867
**IN CANADA:** P.O. Box 609, Fort Erie, Ontario  L2A 5X3

Not valid to current subscribers of Harlequin Historical books.

**Want to try two free books from another line?**
**Call 1-800-873-8635 or visit www.morefreebooks.com.**

* Terms and prices subject to change without notice. Prices do not include applicable taxes. Sales tax applicable in N.Y. Canadian residents will be charged applicable provincial taxes and GST. Offer not valid in Quebec. This offer is limited to one order per household. All orders subject to approval. Credit or debit balances in a customer's account(s) may be offset by any other outstanding balance owed by or to the customer. Please allow 4 to 6 weeks for delivery. Offer available while quantities last.

**Your Privacy:** Harlequin Books is committed to protecting your privacy. Our Privacy Policy is available online at www.eHarlequin.com or upon request from the Reader Service. From time to time we make our lists of customers available to reputable third parties who may have a product or service of interest to you. If you would prefer we not share your name and address, please check here. ☐

HH09R

## Available December 29, 2009

- **THE ROGUE'S DISGRACED LADY**
by **Carole Mortimer**
**(Regency)**
Society gossip has kept Lady Juliet Boyd out of the public eye: all
she really wants is a quiet life. Finally persuaded to accept a summer
house-party invitation, she meets the scandalous Sebastian St. Claire,
a man who makes her feel things, want things, *need* things she's never
experienced before.... But does Sebastian really want Juliet—or just th
truth behind her disgrace?

- **THE KANSAS LAWMAN'S PROPOSAL**
by **Carol Finch**
**(Western)**
Falling in love with dashing lawman Nathan Montgomery was not the
outcome Rachel expected when she joined a Kansas medicine show
wagon! But Dodge City is no place for a single young seamstress, and
despite the secrets that Nate and Rachel hide, they soon begin to need
each other's comfort and protection far more than they anticipated....

- **THE EARL AND THE GOVERNESS**
by **Sarah Elliott**
**(Regency)**
Impoverished, alone and on the run, Isabelle Thomas desperately need
the governess position William Stanton, Earl of Lennox, offers her. Bu
when their passion explodes in a bone-melting kiss, Isabelle knows she
must leave—only the earl has other plans for his innocent governess...

- **PREGNANT BY THE WARRIOR**
by **Denise Lynn**
**(Medieval)**
Lea of Montreau must marry and produce an heir, or lose her lands. Th
headstrong and beautiful lady plots to seduce a particular stranger to
produce an heir—but the stranger is none other than ruggedly handson
Jared of Warehaven—her onetime betrothed childhood sweetheart! Lea
previously rejected Jared, and now he wants his revenge—by marriage